LOVE IN STEREO

BY
JOSÉ F. NODAR

Camden Books Publishing / Spring Farm NSW Australia

Spring Farm NSW Australia / José F. Nodar First Edition

ISBN 978-1-7643714-9-0 – Paperback

ISBN 978-1-7643714-5-2 – E-pub

ISBN 978-1-7643714-6-9 – Audiobook

DEDICATION

In loving memory of my wife,
Miriam Vassallo Nodar,
and her enduring presence.
You are always in my thoughts.
For anyone who's ever loved deeply, lost fully, and still
found
the courage to begin again.

Table of Contents

THE EMPTY RECLINER

Ninety days is a very long time when you're counting them one by one.

Tonight, like most nights, I stand in the lounge and look at your recliner. The leather still keeps the shape of you; a soft bowl in the cushion that remembers your weight better than I do. If I squint, I can almost see the outline of your knees, the place your elbow would settle on the armrest, the little crescent where your thumb used to tap to the rhythm of whatever song I pretended not to like.

I finished dinner 10 minutes ago—"dinner" in this new era being an optimistic word for a plate of scrambled eggs that looked surprised to find themselves on toast—and the house still smells faintly of scorched butter and bravado.

"Good evening, love," I hear myself say, and there it is—the one-sided ritual.

"Weather was wishy-washy today. The sun popped out like it remembered an appointment, then ducked behind the clouds the way I duck behind the shopping trolley when I see a woman with three little kids in tow at Woolies. I saw Walter as well. You remember Walter from down the street. He still wants to tell me about his hernia. Three months, Maureen. Three months of hernia updates."

The recliner answers with dignified silence.

Of course it does. It's furniture.

I shuffle farther into the room, plates clinking as I set them on the coffee table. I'd meant to put them in the dishwasher, but the walk from the dining table to the lounge feels like it is a corridor in a museum now; it requires stopping at the exhibits—your framed photo on the TV stand, your shawl folded on the back of the recliner, the lamp with the switch chain pull you loved.

"The plants are going well," I continue, waving a fork toward the window as if the garden can see me.

"The kookaburras had a committee meeting on the fence this morning. I gave the lemon tree a pep talk. It is still sulking. I think the lemons miss you and your compliments. I told them I was proud of them, and they turned greener just to spite me."

I lower myself onto the edge of my recliner, and it makes that familiar *ssshhck* sound, like a librarian shushing me.

"You'll be delighted to know," I go on, "that tonight's culinary experiment nearly became performance art. I was going for a rustic char on the toast and achieved what critics might call 'molten coal.' The smoke detector applauded me enthusiastically. If I ever wanted to make the front page of the paper, all I would have to do is keep cooking. 'Local Man Redecorates Kitchen with Flames; Claims It's 'Caramelisation'. More on page two.'"

I laugh. It's too loud.

My laughter bounces off the walls and comes back again thinner, as if it's been through the wash and shrunk two sizes. Still, it feels good to let it out. Words need to move, even if they're only walking circles within a single room.

"Claire came by at lunchtime," I say, fiddling with the seam of the cushion beside me. "No announcement, just her knock that sounds like she's auditioning for law enforcement. Never mind the doorbell we installed. She brought a batch of frozen meals with labels written in her boss voice. 'Chicken lasagna: Oven 180°C, 35 min. Do NOT microwave, Dad.' The 'do not' was underlined three times. When she opened the freezer and saw the last lot still there, she clucked like a mother hen. I told her I was letting them age, like fine wine. She didn't think that was as funny as I did."

The recliner holds steady.

It always does.

I like that about it.

Recliners are reliable.

People are too, until suddenly they aren't.

"And Sophie," I continue, "Sophie has been on a crusade to digitise my well-being. She tries to set me up with meditation apps. She said, 'Dad, you just breathe, and the phone does the rest.' I asked her how breathing was going to fix the fact that the left side of the bed refuses to warm up. She told me to imagine warmth. I told her I'd rather have you. She hugged me and then suggested the *Calm* app again. I said, 'Fine, but I'm not paying a subscription to be told how to inhale.' She said there's a free trial. So that's something. If tranquillity doesn't take, at least it won't cost me."

I picture your smile then—the one that started at one corner and ambled across your face like a cat deciding to forgive a human.

There's a pause where your giggle would fit perfectly—the tiny snort you hated and I adored. The room tries to make it up to you with the hum of the fridge, but it doesn't quite get it right.

"Daniel rang on his way home. He said I should get a dog. A rescue dog at that. A companion with paws. I told him the last thing this house needs is another creature who stares at me while I eat. He laughed and said a dog would get me walking more. I told him I already walk over ten thousand steps a day per my Fitbit, plus I go round and round the kitchen table after the smoke alarm goes off. He said that didn't count." I settle back into my recliner and let my shoulders drop.

I reach across the coffee table and straighten the remote controls the way you used to, lining them up lighthouse-small, bigger, biggest. The ritual is part tidiness and part Morse code for the universe; a way of tapping out my message to you: *I remember. I remember.*

"I know what they're doing, my love," I whisper. "They're worried. They think if they keep me busy enough, I'll forget that the house learned how to echo."

I look up at the ceiling, at the way the evening light paints a soft bruise against the architrave. "They don't say it like that. They say practical things. Freezer meals. Apps. Dogs. They're trying to fill in the missing half with items, as if I were a pantry shelf, and if you stack enough tins, the space stops being space."

My voice goes a little wobbly on 'space'. I cough and pretend it was a crumb.

"Three months," I say, and the number feels like a small, heavy thing in my chest.

"Ninety days. Thirteen weeks. Hell, an entire season. Everyone says firsts are the hardest. First night, first week, first grocery run without you next to me calling out the list we wrote.

"The first time I turned to make a joke during the news and remembered that you already knew it somehow. The first time I washed the sheets and had to fold the fitted sheet. I had to decide whether or not to give up trying to do them the way you did, and in the end I just threw them in the linen closet and closed the door. It's all a string of tiny firsts stapled to the big one. You not being here."

I don't notice that my hands have been moving until I see that I've smoothed the recliner's arm with my palm, the same small circles I used to rub against your skin when you were tense. The leather is cool. My hand is warm. The difference feels like the thesis statement of the last 90 days.

"You're talking to a chair, Josh. Congratulations, you've gone round the bend." I say it aloud because if you confess the joke yourself, no one else gets to.

I even add a flourish, like I'm a magician revealing the rabbit was grief all along. For a second, the absurdity cracks me open, and I grin at the empty room until the grin wobbles and turns into something wetter.

I wipe my eyes with the back of my wrist. "Don't worry," I say to the recliner, "I've taken precautions. I haven't actually started answering for you yet. I figure that's the line. Once I impersonate your voice, you're allowed to come back and haunt me proper."

Silence, again.

The house is magnificent in doing that.

The clock ticks time away as if it's eating something.

I try a different tack.

"You'll be pleased to know I watered the inside plants exactly the way you taught me—two cups on Sundays, one on Wednesdays, compliments whispered at least twice a week. I told them that your dresses always make this room happier, and they sighed and pretended not to care. The plants out front are a triumph. Even the neighbours said so, and you know how much of a paid compliment miser they are. The lawn, however, has gone freelance. It's staging a coup. I may have to put on a suit to mow it, just so it knows I mean business."

I glance toward the bookshelf, at the glass jar in the corner with the little notes we used to write to each other—tiny IOUs for later. Even from this distance I can read the top one: 'Owe you a slow dance when the weather turns.' Your handwriting is slanted and assured. Another says, 'If we ever get a dog, you're on poop duty.' I snort. "See? Even from beyond the jar, you and Daniel are in cahoots."

I pick one slip at random and unfold it. "Rain check the water tank to make sure it is flowing correctly," it says. I close it carefully and put it back. There are some checks you keep forever.

On the TV stand, the frame with your photo leans a little. I straighten it. You are laughing at something to the left of the camera—probably me. Your hair is wind-tangled, and your eyes are wide open, as if this is the shot where you took the world into them and kept it there. I used to think photographs trapped a moment. Now I think they release it, minute by minute, like a slow infusion into whoever's looking.

"The kids are good," I tell the recliner, because I don't want to lie to you with anything but omissions. "Claire is tired of being competent. She tries not to let me see, but her shoulders tell on her. Sophie is earnest as a sunrise and hides her fear inside advice. Daniel, he wears his grief like a jacket two sizes too big and insists it fits fine. They're all looking over at me and deciding which screws to tighten, but they haven't looked at themselves yet. I keep wanting to tell them you would be proud of them for caring, and proud of me for pretending I don't need it."

I walk to the patio door. The sky is peeling itself into evening—indigo at the top, apricot at the edges.

I rest my forehead against the cool glass and watch the neighbour's cat decide to own our backyard one step at a time.

"I insist I'm fine," I say, and the glass fogs a little where my breath hits it. "I say it the way people say 'bless you' after a sneeze. Automatic, polite, and mostly for the benefit of the person who did the sneezing. But the truth, Maureen—you know this already—life without you feels like half of me has gone missing. Not amputated, exactly. More like your half slipped out to the kitchen for a cup of coffee and forgot to come back, and now I'm stuck here holding the conversation on my own. I miss you heaps my love, and I hope you know that."

I turn from the door and my eyes land on the recliner again—the indentation, the small rip in the right-hand seam, the blanket folded over the back like a shoulder shawl. It looks comfortable and a little smug. If a recliner could raise an eyebrow, this one would judge me gently.

"I keep thinking you're in the bedroom," I confess. "That if I say your name the right way, you'll say 'What?' in that tone that meant 'Yes, I'm listening, even if I'm pretending, I'm not'. I keep thinking the story's just paused and if I find the remote, I can get it going again. And then there are nights like this where I realise it didn't pause—it changed channels without asking me—and I'm here trying to follow a plot I didn't sign up for."

I sit on the edge of your recliner's arm the way I used to when you were dozing, and I had something trivial to share. Those trivialities were most of what we traded and, in hindsight, my best currency. The leather gives, and I can smell the ghost of your shampoo, or maybe it's only memory make-believe to be a scent so it can get closer.

"I'm going to learn how to make your roast chicken properly. I will stand just where you stood and talk to the pan as if it's a skittish animal, and I will baste the way you did, with patience and unreasonable optimism. And yes, I will probably set off the smoke alarm again, but I'll get there. I'll keep going until the house smells right."

I stay like that for a long time, just breathing, listening to the tick of the clock and the faraway hush of the night. If I close my eyes, I can feel the weight of your hand on my shoulder, which is nonsense of the most precious kind.

Finally, I stand. "Goodnight, my love," I say to the indentation, to the blanket, to the air that still remembers the shape of your laughter.

I collect my plate and fork and make my way back to the kitchen. Halfway there, I stop and look back into the lounge. For a second, just a second, I imagine the recliner will rise and follow me, the way you would, rolling your eyes and saying,

"Did you soak the pan, Joshua?"; putting my name into extra syllables so it can carry the scold and the smile at once.

The recliner doesn't move.

Of course it doesn't.

Recliners are reliable.

In the kitchen, the pan waits in the sink, with a black ring where the eggs met their fate. I turn on the tap and let the water run until it's hot enough to mean business. Steam rises, blooms, disappears. I set the plate down, pick up the sponge, and start the small, ordinary work of making something ready for tomorrow.

THE JUMPER

That afternoon began the way all my afternoons since had. The way they did when you were learning a new life: with chores you invented to keep from sitting still.

I told myself I was 'organising the wardrobe'. It sounded official, like I might uncover a filing system behind the shoeboxes and winter clothes. In truth, I was rummaging half like an archaeologist, half like a raccoon; pulling out old boxes and muttering about the kind of dust that went directly for the nostrils and made every memory sneeze when you touched it.

Silly, right?

The sunlight slanted across the bedroom window and hit Maureen's dresser, turning the floating motes into a snow globe someone had shaken too hard. I had three boxes open on the bed: one for 'Keep,' one for 'Donate to Mother Hubbard,' and one for 'Not Sure Where These Came From."

'Not Sure Where These Came From,' was winning.

It contained, at last count, a tie with tiny saxophones on it (what had I been proving?), a pair of socks with toes (whose idea of comfort was partitioned digits?), and a T-shirt from a conference in 2000 that proudly declared 'I survived Y2K'. I had not survived good taste, apparently.

In the back corner of the wardrobe, behind the suitcase we only used when we were feeling optimistic about airplane seats, there was a shallow cardboard box with a split lid. It had an almost-visible aura of something I'd ignored on purpose. I dragged it out, knees protesting, and had to sit on the floor to catch my breath. (You'd think grief would at least pay rent for how much space it was taking up in my lungs.)

I pried the lid back and stared into a pile that could have doubled as a museum exhibit: 'Josh's Poor Choices: A Retrospective.'

It contained a mixtape I'd made Maureen from the radio (complete with reckless DJ interruptions), a Polaroid of me in a haircut that could get me arrested today, and then—buried like the punchline to an old joke—my old Georgia Tech jumper. I'd never attended Georgia Tech as a student while I lived in the state of Georgia in the USA all those years ago, but I'd really liked the yellowjacket mascot, so I bought the jumper on a lark.

Now it was a shade of what it had been. Threadbare, a small hole in the sleeve, and faded to an almost comical shade of sick blue—the particular hue of something that used to be proud and had been through enough wash cycles to forget its original dream.

I laughed aloud. "My, my; this old thing," I said, lifting it as if it might confess something from my past.

The knit sagged between my fingers in weary lines. I could almost hear Maureen groan. She'd always called it 'The Relic.' "It has seen things," she'd say, pinching it at arm's length, "and none of them good."

I held it to my chest and closed my eyes.

It smelled of cedar from the small block Maureen used to tuck among the jumpers. Underneath it, or maybe above it— these things weren't faithful to physics—was the ghost of something warmer, the scent I associated with winter and your laugh.

Without thinking, I tugged it over my head.

Old muscle memory made it easy; the jumper knew my shoulders the way a well-worn chair knew a favourite sigh. The knit fell against my ribs with a scratch that almost hurt and thereby convincingly doing its job. I checked the sleeve out of habit—the hole had grown teeth—and then I turned to the wardrobe mirror to see how stupid I looked.

That was when I heard her.

"Josh, for heaven's sake; that thing still exists? I told you to burn it in 1992."

I nearly toppled backward over the shoebox mound. My heart did something unhelpful and acrobatic in my chest.

I spun, because of course I spun; because how else did you greet a voice that belonged to the person you had been missing in every molecule?

There she was.

Not solid—not the way the bed was solid, or the way a cupboard door would teach your forehead about certainty if you stood up too fast.

But she was *there*: faint, translucent, smiling as though she'd simply walked in from the kitchen with a cup of coffee and the expression she used when I told a story that wanted pruning. The light from the window seemed to pass through her and then, thinking better of it, clung for a second to the shape of her shoulder before wavering.

"Maureen," I said, except what came out was any sound that a man whose name had fallen off a cliff and was currently tumbling through him on its way down could make.

"Hello, my love," she said, as ordinary as weather. "Well, now. Look at that jumper. It's learnt to haunt you before I did."

I reached out. I didn't plan to; in the same way one doesn't plan to blink or to hope. My hand shook. I lifted it to her shoulder, to the place where I'd rested my palm a thousand times in a thousand kitchens; the place that had carried bags and babies and a life with me. My fingers met the air. They kept going and went nowhere. Her shoulder was a mirage with a familiar outline.

I made a small noise. It tried to be a laugh and sat down, exhausted, as a sob.

Maureen cocked her head the way she did when she was calibrating tenderness.

"Oh, Josh," she said, and my name broke twice—once for the ache and once for the joy. "Don' t push it, darling. I'm here differently." Maureen smiled, and there were her teeth; imperfect with that little gap, and so dazzling. There was her mouth; a shape I'd forever ago memorised. There was the dimple that showed up to throw confetti when the smile got too pleased with itself.

I tried again. "Has a lack of sleep finally made me start hallucinating?"

"*Are* you hallucinating?" Maureen glanced pointedly at my reflection. "Not with that jumper on."

It was absurd.

It was impossible.

It was so perfectly Maureen to arrive in the middle of a mess and choose, for her first words from beyond whatever beyond is, to scold my wardrobe.

The joy and the heartbreak of the moment collided like strangers in a doorway. I laughed. The laugh ran headlong into tears, and both of them made a choking sound of such awkwardness that if anyone else had been present, we all might have agreed to call it a musical experiment.

"You told me to burn it," I managed, wiping my eyes with the heel of my hand. "You did; you did. You staged interventions. You held backyard tribunals."

"I had witnesses," Maureen said. "Ask Claire. She'll remember. I filed petitions with the Domestic Court of Common Sense. The judge—me—ruled it a danger to taste and possibly to health."

"It has sentimental value."

"Josh, it has smells."

I made a noise that wanted to be a chuckle and didn't quite land. "You're here," I said, which felt like placing a flag on a planet that might move underfoot. "You're actually here."

I could see the glossy streak of the wardrobe behind her, the blur of the duvet through her elbows. The physics made no promises, and yet the personhood did. What made up 'Maureen' in this moment had nothing to do with atoms and everything to do with the tilt of the head, the cadence of a sentence, the way she appraised my foolishness with her affection set to 'glow.'

"I am," Maureen said simply. "You put that thing on and—well. I could hardly resist the opportunity."

"Is this—" The question went sprawling. "Have you been around?"

Her expression did a quick little dance—regret partnering with mischief. "Some," she said. "It's hard to explain. Time is like a cat. It sits on you and purrs, and sometimes it wanders off and you're not sure how long it's been gone. Today, it brought me to the wardrobe and meowed at your jumper."

"Time is like a cat," I repeated, because my brain was clinging to the nearest sturdy metaphor. "Damn it, of course it is."

She glanced down, or through, at my hands. "You've been rummaging."

"Organising," I lied with a straight face. "Archiving. Curating. I found the mixtape. The one with the DJ who loved to sabotage poetry."

"Oh, he tried," she said, a glimmer of nostalgia lighting her from within. "You promised me a song, and then he bulldozed in to announce the price of ham at Woolies."

"I compensated by writing you the lyrics. On the back of a Woolies catalogue." I swallowed. The lump in my throat was ridiculous and very real in temperature. "I didn't throw it out."

"I know," Maureen said, and the way she said it—soft, smug, and sure—undid me with a gentle hand. "You kept everything that mattered and half the things that didn't."

We stood like that—or rather, I stood, and you did whatever the verb was for being present without making dents. The bedroom breathed around us. I wanted to memorise this moment not because it was spectacular, but because it was so ordinary—our shared specialty.

"Say something else," I blurted, suddenly afraid that if we didn't keep words airborne, they'd fall like birds, and the moment would be a single wingbeat. "Anything. Tease me. Tell me off. Tell me to change the sheets properly."

She made a small, delighted face. "Change the sheets properly, Josh."

I laughed. "You can't smuggle four words and my name from beyond."

"Watch me," she said, and did.

I stepped closer without thinking and stopped at the tremble in the air that was Maureen. And because stillness might have broken me in two, I turned back to the mirror. We met there, all three of us: me in a jumper that should have taken its superannuation when John Howard was still around, her smudged into the world like a careful pencil line, and the space between—busy, shimmering, somehow populated by everything we had ever said and not said.

"Do you hurt, baby?" I asked reflexively because that had been the question that had ruled our last months. It leapt out now out of habit, tripping on its own urgency.

Maureen's eyes softened. "No," she said, and the syllable was such a mercy that I had to sit down on the closed lid of the suitcase. "It's different now."

"Different how?"

"You know how laughter feels when you're already crying?" She tilted her head, looking for the right corner to enter my understanding. "How do both things happen at once and make a new thing? It's like that. Only bigger. And quieter."

I nodded as if I could imagine it. Maybe part of me could.

We tried small talk because big talk threatened to collapse under its own honesty. I told her about the plants. She told me the neighbour's cat had been cheating on our porch with our cushion. I asked if she could hold anything. She lifted her hand toward the wardrobe handle, and it flickered, the handle twitched, and then nothing. She made a face. "I'm not very good at physics, Josh. You'll have to give me time."

"Time is like a cat," I reminded her, because one of us should remember her metaphors.

She glanced at the hole in my sleeve. "We could start," she said, tone brightening, "by not wearing that in public."

I made a wounded noise. "The jumper and I have been through a lot. Heartbreaks from old girlfriends—all of which you know, because I told you—and of course cheap beer."

"So now it's earned a dignified retirement," she said briskly. "You can fold it and give it a speech. Thank it for its service. Present it with a watch."

"It is a watch," I said, pointing to a frayed cuff. "It tells the time when it was always two in the morning."

Maureen smiled that smile that told me she'd let me have the joke as a consolation prize. "Wear it here, then," she allowed. "In this room. Where it can't mortify me. For comfort, I mean. If you... want comfort."

There it was again, the thin wire between joy and ache. "I do," I admitted too quickly. "I really do."

We tested boundaries. We learned I could hear Maureen best when I was calm; that if I spiralled in thought, she fuzzed at the edges. We learned that if I took the jumper off—purely as an experiment—and her outline dimmed like a light on a theatre cue. I put it back on so fast I nearly dislocated a shoulder.

She laughed a little, shook her head, and said, "No, love. It's not a lamp. I'm not in the fabric. I'm here because, well, just because."

"Because?"

"Because we are very persistent people," she said, and the 'we' made my ribs feel like a bell.

There were questions I didn't ask—about where she was when she wasn't here, about whether there was a door and if it had a draft. There would be a time for that, or there wouldn't, and either way this hour was already so much more than I had thought the universe would hand back.

I stood up, resisting the urge to reach again. "Can I make you a coffee?" I asked because what else do you do when your dead wife shows up and the thing you want is impossible, but your hands still feel like they should do something kind? "I know you can't drink it, but I could set it in your activity room. For tradition."

"I would like that," Maureen said solemnly. "And then I can sit here and critique your coffee-making skills. From a moral standpoint."

"You always did," I said, moving toward the kitchen. I stopped with my hand on the door frame and turned back, suddenly certain that if I looked away, she might wear off like chalk in rain. "Maureen?"

"Mmm?"

"I'm frightened," I said. The truth was small, unadorned, and spilled out of me like a coin I'd been clenching too tight.

"I know," you said. She took a step closer that made no sound at all. "Me too, in a way. But look at us. We're doing it."

"Doing what?"

"Continuing." She smiled. "Rudely, stubbornly, with questionable knitwear."

I laughed, and the laugh held itself up on its own legs. "Go into the activity room," I said as I opened the door. "Stay," I said, a plea watching its manners, "while I make the coffee."

"I will."

Down in the kitchen, I filled the kettle and listened to it gather itself. The house felt different; the echo had an answer. I warmed her favourite mug, the one with the chip that looked like Tasmania, and placed it on the bench with mine. When the kettle clicked, I poured, and the steam rose and curled like a cat's tail in the air.

Carrying both mugs, I went into the activity room, where Maureen did all her sewing, arts, and crafts, and balanced both coffee mugs as if they were sacred. I half expected the room to be empty on principle, to have to relearn how to stand with the absence. But when I turned in, Maureen was there, by the sewing machine, precise as a memory and as shaky as a heartbeat.

"Oh, Joshua," she said when she saw the mugs. "You remembered my mug."

"Supervision helps," I said. I set her mug on the workbench, just to the left of the sewing machine, and mine beside it. I stood next to her and watched the coffee steam rise.

The jumper held me by the ribs and, for the first time in whatever the new units were that measured grief, I felt warmer than the fabric could account for.

"I told you to burn it," she murmured again because jokes were our rosary.

"I know," I said gently. "But if I had not, what would you have had to make fun of today?"

"Oh, love," she said, smiling so much I thought the room might lift a little. "You underestimate me."

THE PROOF IS IN THE JUMPER

"Maureen, come to the bedroom for a second," I said.

I sat on the edge of the bed; the jumper hung loose on my shoulders and my heart still clanged like a dropped saucepan. Maureen was right there—*right there*—looking like she had stepped out of thin air with her familiar smirk. My brain, meanwhile, was staggering around trying to catch up.

"How… how is this even happening?" I asked, my voice half plea, half accusation. "You're here, but you're not. You're talking to me, but—how?"

Maureen tilted her head the way she always did when a question was impossible, but she wasn't about to let that ruin her day. "I don't know, love. One minute I wasn't, and the next, I was. You put on that ridiculous jumper, and poof! Instant haunting."

"That's not an explanation," I muttered.

"It's the only one I've got. You wanted an afterlife PowerPoint? Sorry, Josh, they didn't hand out manuals at the pearly gates. Assuming there were gates. For all I know, it was just a cosmic bus stop."

I rubbed at my face, trying to press some sense back into it. A mad thought struck me. "Wait," I said, tugging at the hem of the jumper. "Let me just test something."

"Josh—"

Too late. I yanked the jumper over my head, static crackling in my hair, and before I could blink, she was gone. The room sagged under its own emptiness.

"Maureen?" I whispered. The walls stared back.

My chest tightened with a sharp, familiar ache. Of course. Of course, it had been a trick of grief, a conjuring from memory. I'd broken myself open so hard that my mind had finally staged a coup.

I shoved the jumper back over my head, my hands clumsy, desperate. The wool scraped my skin as if it disapproved of my haste. And then—

"There you are," she said, rolling her eyes as if she'd just watched me forget the kettle again. "Well, aren't you a clever detective? Elementary, my dear idiot."

I let out a laugh that came out more like a bark. Relief and horror jostled for elbow room in my chest. "So that's it? Jumper on, you're here. Jumper off, you vanish. What am I supposed to make of that?"

"That heaven has a sense of humour," she said without missing a beat. She leaned back against the wardrobe as if she owned the place. "I begged you for years to throw that thing out, and instead it's turned into my calling card. God has to be a comedian."

I tugged at the sleeve, staring at the frayed hole, the miserable colour. "You're tethered to my least attractive piece of clothing."

Maureen grinned, wicked and proud. "Well, you always needed me to keep you humble."

I buried my face in my hands, half-laughing, half-groaning. "This can't be real. Either I'm losing my mind, or my marriage vows now extend to knitwear. 'Till death and the jumper do us part.'"

"You're not crazy," she said, and for a moment her voice softened. "And even if you are, you're my kind of crazy."

I looked up at her—translucent, faint, but so very her—and I didn't know whether to be grateful or to ring the nearest asylum and book myself a room. Both options seemed reasonable.

She winked. "Don't worry, love. If you do check yourself in, I'll still be here. Sitting in the corner, mocking your hospital gown."

That was Maureen through and through: still able to turn my unravelling into a joke, still able to make me feel, in one breath, that I was both entirely doomed and somehow safe.

And for the first time in 90 days, I didn't feel completely alone.

MAUREEN'S BANTER IS BACK

The strangest thing about seeing your dead wife in your bedroom isn't the shock. The shock is brief, loud, and a moment that leaves your heart stumbling like it missed a step. It's what comes after that's stranger: the way your body remembers the rhythm of her presence, the way your mouth finds its way back into the same banter as though 90 days of silence were only a long breath.

I was in the lounge still wearing the jumper—my new and unwanted ticket to haunting—and sat fiddling with the chewed cuff, when Maureen, translucent and smug, tilted her head at me.

"Josh," she said. "Can I ask something?"

"Sure," I said.

"What have you done to your face, by the way?"

"What about my face?" I asked, already wary.

"The beard is patchy as a second-hand quilt. Honestly, you look like you've been mugged by a lawnmower and lost." Her lips mocked me.

"Well, forgive me. Ghosts don't exactly have salon appointments, Maureen. You can't exactly lecture me from the other side about personal grooming."

Her eyes sparkled. "Excuse me, mister 'I bought one razor in 2009 and decided it was a family heirloom.' I've had opinions about your facial hair since our second date. Death hasn't changed that."

The words landed with such ordinary weight that for a heartbeat I forgot everything else. It was just us; the familiar sparring, the laughter tucked behind every barb. The sound that came out of me was genuine laughter—loud, rough, shoulders shaking—the kind I hadn't made in weeks.

"Maybe I'll grow it out," I said, stroking my chin theatrically. "Become one of those mysterious widowers with a Gandalf beard. Women will stop me in the street and ask if I've seen their lost hobbits."

"You'll never get past patchy, love. Your chin has been on strike since I met you."

"Harsh."

"True."

I laughed again, for she was right, and for a few golden seconds, I wasn't a man three months widowed in a jumper too ugly to live. I was just Josh, married to Maureen and the target of her loving mockery.

But muscle memory is a tricky traitor.

Without thinking, I stood, my arms opening automatically. I reached for her the way I had a thousand times—when she came in from the garden, when she was carrying shopping bags, when she was half-asleep getting out of the recliner. My body braced for weight, for warmth, for the solid truth of her shoulder under my hand.

And I stumbled forward into nothing.

The momentum nearly toppled me onto the floor.

I caught myself, my laugh crumbling into a broken sound I couldn't disguise. The sound you never mean to make in front of anyone.

Her face shifted instantly, her teasing falling away. She stepped closer—though it meant nothing—and her voice was quiet. "Josh…"

I couldn't look at her.

My hands and shoulders trembled.

"Damn it, Maureen. This is not enough," I choked. "You're here, and you're not. I can hear you, I can see you, but I can't hold you, and holding you is what I want the most."

Maureen's expression softened into something that cracked me wide open. Her voice was a whisper, the kind that made your bones lean in to listen. "I'm here, love. Just differently."

I wiped at my face with the sleeve of the jumper, leaving a dark, damp patch on the wool.

She noticed of course.

"Well," she said gently, "at least you've finally found a use for that monstrosity. Absorbent."

The joke landed exactly right, and somehow my sobs collapsed into laughter again. Ridiculous, tangled, messy laughter, but laughter all the same. It felt like grief and comedy were arm-wrestling inside me, neither quite winning.

I sat down in my recliner, catching my breath. She was smiling. "There," she said. "That's more like you."

I shook my head, still chuckling weakly. "You always had the worst timing."

"Timing is everything, my love."

She settled herself—or appeared to—on her recliner, which she clearly intended to claim even in ghost form.

"Besides, if I waited until you were dignified, I'd be waiting forever."

I gestured at the surrounding clutter: half-used tissues, the tower of books on the floor that hadn't been touched, the layer of dust creeping in on the TV stand. "I suppose you're here to comment on the housekeeping too?"

She sniffed, inspecting the piles with her usual raised eyebrow. "I die for three months, and you forget how to tidy up. Look at that mess. Dirty as a politician. Do you even remember how to fold a fitted sheet?"

"No. You fold them yourself, then," I retorted, a grin tugging at my mouth.

Her smile flickered with mischief. "I would, if physics didn't insist on being such a spoilsport."

The laugh that bubbled out of me was almost giddy. "Do you realise what this is? 90 days without you and we're back to arguing about sheets."

"Yes," she said simply. "Isn't it wonderful?"

It was.

It was absurd and heartbreaking and so wonderfully, achingly ordinary.

We sat together like that for a while. She teased my beard again, demanded I dust the top of the wardrobe ("You've created a whole new ecosystem up there"), and accused me of keeping the blinds crooked on purpose. I shot back that she was still bossy even without a pulse, and she just grinned and said, "Some things transcend mortality."

The ache never went away—how could it?—but it threaded itself around the laughter instead of swallowing it whole.

At one point, I reached for her again, even though I knew better. My hand passed through, of course, but this time I steadied myself, didn't stumble.

She observed me.

"Don't," she whispered. "Don't torture yourself like that."

"I can't help it."

"I know." She smiled softly. "That's why I came back. To help you try."

And then, because she could never let me wallow for long, she added, "But also to save your children from your beard. You're welcome."

I threw my head back and laughed, the sound loud enough to rattle the glass in the picture frames.

For the first time since the funeral, I felt more laughter than heartbreak.

And for the first time in 90 days, I didn't feel entirely alone in the room.

TABLE SET FOR TWO

By late afternoon, the house had settled into that pre-evening hush that always made you reach for the TV remote. I didn't. The TV was booby-trapped these days; one news story and I was crawling under the table like a shell-shocked meerkat. Instead, I set about the noble work of dinner, which in my hands was less 'culinary art' and more 'chemical experiment performed by a distracted man in knitwear'."

I kept the jumper on.

Of course I did. Damned right I did.

If my choices were (A) look like I lost a fight with a washing machine but have Maureen, or (B) dress like a human and risk silence—I'd wear this sick blue relic to a royal wedding.

"Right," I announced to the kitchen. "We're aiming for edible."

From the master bedroom door, Maureen gave a dignified snort. "Aim higher. 'Recognisable as food' should be our baseline."

I held up a saucepan like a shield. "Pasta. How hard can pasta be?"

"Famous last words," she said, perching—appearing to perch—on the dining table where the fruit bowl sulked with two brown bananas and a pear old enough to vote.

I filled a pot and set it on the stovetop.

The water's slow consent to boil felt like a mercy; at least physics still returned my calls. I consulted a packet of penne as if it might reveal marital wisdom. "10 minutes," I read aloud.

"Or until you forget," Maureen murmured.

"Not tonight, my love, for tonight I have company."

I set a timer like a responsible adult and rummaged for sauce options. There was a jar of something tomato-adjacent, a handful of olives, and half an onion that had seen better days. "We'll do a sort of Mediterranean theme," I said bravely.

Maureen left the table and leaned in—she didn't cast a shadow, but somehow, she still had a presence—and studied the onion. "You know one has a will."

"They all do."

I began chopping with what I hoped looked like confidence and what probably looked like a man negotiating with a vegetable.

"Remember our first unit?" I said, flicking onion to the pan with a flourish that impressed no one. "We had that wobbly stove and the frying pan with a personality disorder."

"You made me an omelette that could withstand artillery fire," she said, smiling. "And I married you, anyway."

"Because of the omelette," I insisted.

"Despite the omelette."

The onion hissed in butter. I felt absurdly proud.

I let the pride sit on my tongue a moment, then let it melt—because the genuine pleasure wasn't the sound of cooking, it was the commentary.

90 days of silence had transformed into this bubbling, teasing domesticity, and I wanted to drink it like water.

"Wine?" I asked, opening the fridge.

"For you," she said. "I can't exactly enjoy a Pinot in my current state."

"I can pour it and leave it there," I offered.

"And watch you drink two glasses to make up for it? Tempting, but you know how giddy you get with more than one glass."

I poured only one glass.

The timer ticked down from seven minutes. I stirred the onions, added the jarred sauce, a splash of water, a fistful of olives, and—in a burst of optimism Maureen would have mocked when breathing—a few leaves from the wilted basil plant on the windowsill. The sauce looked passable. The pasta softened obediently.

For once, the smoke alarm remained silent and aloof, like an aristocrat in exile.

"Set the table," Maureen said, as naturally as if she were reaching for the cutlery drawer herself. "Properly. Napkins. Plates not in a precarious tower. No 'bachelor chic' ."

I pulled two plates from the cupboard.

My hand hesitated.

Then I set both down.

One for me and one for her.

My chest did that painful swelling thing—the way a laugh sometimes turns its ankle and becomes a sob.

She noticed. "It's alright," she said, more gently. "I like the ritual. Do it."

I did.

Two plates, two forks, two spoons, two glasses (though only one with wine). I even put a third little dish for grated cheese, because I'm nothing if not a man with delusions of grandeur. I lit a candle from the drawer—the short, stout kind you buy for power outages—and set it between us.

It felt corny and perfect.

The timer sang.

I drained the pasta without incident, which I felt deserved a standing ovation, then married sauce to penne with the hesitant grace of a widower officiating his first wedding. I brought the bowls to the table and sat. Across from me, Maureen arranged herself in her chair as if she could feel the cushion.

She couldn't.

We both pretended.

I took my first bite.

It was fine.

Not a triumph, not a war crime.

"Well?" I asked, delighted to have an audience again. "Marks out of 10?"

"For not burning down the house: eight," she said, eyes twinkling. "For seasoning: five. For the presentation: darling, you ladled the pasta like you were filling potholes."

"I was going for rustic."

"Well, you achieved roadwork."

We fell into the old rhythms so quickly it felt like waking up into a life I'd only been dreaming. I ate slowly to make the moment last longer. I told her about the plants' progress, and she scolded me for forgetting to trim the dead geranium heads.

I complained about the prices at Woolies. She said that everything is going up—learn to budget. We argued about whether the salt sat closer to me or to her (it was in front of me; I slid it across anyway).

At one point I lifted my wineglass, and she lifted her empty hand, and we did the motion of clinking.

No sound.

Still, the gesture felt complete.

"You know what this is?" I said, twirling pasta the way I'd watched her do a hundred times and never mastered. "It's ridiculous how happy I am right now."

"Ridiculous is our brand," she said. "Besides, you're wearing the jumper. There's only so much dignity available."

I looked down at the sick blue knit, at the loose threads, the hole that had looked like a cartoon mouth permanently surprised at its own existence. "I suppose dinner theatre requires a costume."

"Oh, it does."

We were in the middle of comparing notes on whether the neighbour's new hedge was a topiary or a cry for help when footsteps clattered on the front steps and the door knocked in Sophie's impatient rhythm.

"Dad?" she called, letting herself in without waiting, as she always had. Sophie's voice has urgency even when she's ordering a coffee. "I brought you that mindfulness brochure— they're doing a free intro tonight."

My fork froze halfway to my mouth. Across from me, Maureen's eyebrows sprung up in a gleeful arc. "Showtime," she whispered.

Sophie rounded the corner of the kitchen and stopped. Her eyes took in the candle, the two plates, the two napkins, the extra glass.

Her gaze sharpened.

"Dad," she said slowly and carefully, like words might spook me, "are you expecting someone?"

"Ah." I glanced at Maureen, who was openly enjoying herself. "Tradition," I babbled. "Just keeping traditions alive."

Sophie looked at the empty chair across from me. It had the infuriating innocence of furniture. "Two plates is a strong tradition."

"I over-served," I said. "You know me. Generous to a fault."

"Yeah, right?"

She dropped her tote on the kitchen counter and approached as if I were a wild animal she didn't want to startle. She reached the table and sniffed.

"Smells good," she conceded, surprised.

"It's food," I said brightly. "Recognisable as such."

Her eyes flicked to the jumper. "You've kept that."

"Sentimental value," I said.

"And it smells," Maureen added, prim as a judge.

I choked on a laugh and coughed to disguise it.

Sophie handed me a paper pamphlet as if it might defuse a bomb.

"It's an eight-week series," she said, tapping the schedule. "Breathwork, gentle movement, a community of people dealing with grief. It might help."

Maureen leaned toward me, conspiratorial. "Ask if they offer a module on 'Not Setting Pasta on Fire.'"

I took the pamphlet and nodded like a bobblehead. "Thank you. Very thoughtful."

Sophie's gaze slid back to the extra place setting. "Dad," she said, softer now, "we can set a place for Mum sometimes. If that helps. Some people do that. But it might hurt more. I don't know." She swallowed.

Across the table, Maureen's face softened. "She's trying so hard," she whispered. "Be kind."

"I know," I breathed, then realised I'd said it aloud. Sophie tipped her head.

"You know…?"

"I know you're trying," I blurted. "And I appreciate it. I do."

She exhaled, relieved to have landed somewhere. "Good. Because I also brought this."

From her tote she produced a small bright object like a toy spaceship. "An essential oil diffuser. Calm blend. Lavender, chamomile, something called 'Moon Water' which is probably just distilled marketing."

Maureen clapped her spectral hands. "Moon Water! We've reached the crystal era."

Sophie plugged it in.

In seconds, the kitchen began exhaling a polite mist that smelled like a spa trying not to offend anyone. "I can stay," she said. "We could watch something. Or I could just sit, you know, in the lounge, while you finish."

"You don't have to, sweetheart," I said, maybe too quickly. She heard it and flinched. I softened my voice. "But thank you."

She nodded, awkward, hovering.

Her eyes went back to the empty recliner.

"Sometimes," she said, almost a whisper, "I talk to her too. In my car. I say goodnight and please don't let me forget the parking meter, and sometimes I hear, I don't know, not words. Just like a nudge."

She winced as if she'd confessed to shoplifting. "I sound mad."

"No," I said, throat closing. "You sound like my daughter."

She blinked fast.

"Okay." She straightened, found the thread of her mission again. "Well. I'll leave you to it. But, Dad?" She glanced at the candle, at the two plates, at me in that jumper. "If you ever want to eat with someone who actually eats, call me. Or Claire. Or Daniel. We can bring more than a brochure. You know we worry."

"I will," I said. And I meant it.

Sophie squeezed my shoulder—her hand warm, real— and left in a swirl of lavender steam and paperwork.

The front door shut. The house exhaled.

Across from me, Maureen rose from her chair with a theatrical flourish.

"I like her diffuser," she said. "It makes the kitchen smell like a yoga teacher."

"Moon Water," I said. "Fantastic, we have now crossed into astrology."

"Careful. If Claire brings crystals, we'll have to stage an intervention from both sides of the veil."

I sank back into my chair.

My pulse slowed.

The candle flickered, proud of having gotten through an entire cameo. The pasta had cooled into a more stubborn form of itself, but I kept eating because putting the fork down felt like admitting to the universe that it had won.

"She worries," Maureen said, softer. "They all do. And they're right to."

"I know, babe. I know."

I stared at the empty glass I'd set for her. The absence remained an absence no matter how cleverly we joked around it. "I know," I said again, this time to both of us.

We ate—well, I ate, and she commented—and the conversation drifted to safer banks: the neighbour's new car (red; midlife crisis), the sunburnt patch on the lawn (accusatory), the way the diffuser made our home smell like a small, manageable hope.

At one point I lifted the wine and gestured, and Maureen lifted nothing and met me in the gesture, and the click that didn't happen sounded anyway in the part of me that had learned to hear with memory.

"Do you remember?" I asked. "The night the power went out, and we made that ridiculous candlelit picnic on the balcony of the unit with whatever we had in the pantry? Tinned tuna, stale crackers, pickles, and chocolate chips?"

"And we declared it *haute* cuisine," she said. "We were poor and happy and absolutely certain we were geniuses."

"We sure as hell were," I said, and to my surprise it didn't hurt to say it. It glowed, the way a far-off window did when you drove past at night and wondered who lived there.

When the bowls were mostly history, I gathered the plates.

Habit made me reach across for hers, and habit reminded me halfway that there was nothing to gather. I flinched, then grinned, set my plate on hers so I could carry two at once, and stood.

"Progress," she said, amused. "Efficiency at last."

"At last," I echoed.

We did the washing-up together—me doing and her directing. "Angle the plate," she said. "Place it correctly so more will fit, and then you can run the dishwasher in the morning to take advantage of the solar panels."

"You'd think haunting would change your priorities," I said.

"It has," she said. "I only nag about what matters."

"So, angles matter."

"Cleanliness is next to godliness," she said primly, then ruined it with a grin. "And it also kept you from sulking."

When the last fork stood in the rack like a silver fence, we drifted back to the table. The candle had slumped into itself, a small white crater. I pinched the wick, and it sighed out a ribbon of smoke that curled toward the ceiling as if reading out a last line.

"We did it," I said. "Dinner without incident. Mostly."

"You were charming," she said. "And you didn't burn the garlic, which is growth."

"Would you like dessert?" I asked. "I could put a biscuit on a saucer and call it continental."

She laughed. "I'll watch you eat it and offer notes."

"Sounds romantic."

"It always was."

I fetched two biscuits because I was nothing if not a man determined to pretend properly, and set one on the plate in front of her and one in front of me.

I ate mine in absurdly small bites to make it last.

She narrated the biscuit's feelings about being chosen.

"It's honoured," she said. "It has always hoped to be part of a moment."

When the crumbs were loyal only to the tablecloth, we sat in a silence I didn't rush to fill.

Outside, the sky was finishing the job of darkening itself. The diffuser hummed like a very focused bee.

Somewhere, a neighbour's dog barked loudly.

"I could get used to this," I said at last, quietly. "The talking. The bossing. The togetherness."

"I'm counting on it," she said. "But, Josh?"

"What, honey?"

"Promise me something."

"Depends. Does it involve replacing the jumper?"

"Not tonight."

She tilted her head, and the loving-serious look I'd learned to respect settled into place. "Promise me you'll eat with a person-with-a-pulse sometimes. Claire. Sophie. Daniel. A friend–male, or female, but especially a female, for I know you need female companionship. It doesn't have to be fancy. A toasty sandwich will do. Just in the meatspace, as Daniel would say."

"Meatspace," I repeated, grimacing. "Horrible word."

"Good practice." She smiled. "Promise."

I looked at the spare plate, at the candle crater, at the jumper sleeve fraying like a diagram of time. My throat swelled.

"Sure, I promise," I said. "Sometimes."

"That's my guy."

I cleared away the last traces of our dinner for two: the comedy of a table set for what the world would insist was one.

In the lounge room, our recliners waited with their calm indentations, smug and welcoming. I sat on the lounge with all of its pillows instead and patted the cushion beside me to encourage her.

She came and 'sat,' occupying the space where a person would. I didn' t put my arm around her like my heart and muscle memory itched to. Instead I tucked my hands under my thighs and listened to the house breathe.

"Do you want the radio or the TV?" I asked, tentative.

She shook her head. "Not yet. Let's let the quiet be the noise for a bit."

So, we did.

And if my eyes stung, and if once or twice a laugh burst out of me at absolutely nothing because it felt like a necessary punctuation, well, that was just the new grammar of us: laughter first, ache after, then laughter again.

I fell asleep on the lounge like that: jumper on, diffuser going; my last thought the ridiculous certainty that tomorrow night I'd chop the onion smaller, salt the water more boldly, and set two plates again—because even if only one of us could eat, both of us were hungry.

BLUE JUMPER AND A YELLOW JACKET

I'd just made myself a cup of coffee the colour of a dark afternoon and settled into my recliner—the one that had moulded itself to my grief and also my dodgy right hip— when Claire marched in like a union rep for adult children.

"Family meeting," she announced, already rearranging my coasters.

My eldest had two superpowers: taking charge and making me wipe down surfaces I didn't know existed.

Behind her drifted Daniel, long and lanky, still trying to fold himself into his thirties without creasing, and Sophie, thumb already floating over her phone like a hummingbird over nectar. The look on her face said: say the word 'confusion,' Dad, and I will Google you into a facility by this afternoon.

"I don't recall voting for a family meeting," I said, blowing on my coffee, which bravely refused to cool.

The three of them sat on the lounge, next to me.

Claire sat on the edge, posture like a new ruler. "We noticed some things, Dad."

"'We' noticed?" I asked.

"Claire noticed," Daniel said. "We were told to notice."

Sophie nodded, eyes still on the glow of her screen. "I've got three dementia symptom checklists open, but I'm flexible."

"Excellent," I said. "A flexible diagnosis. Very modern."

From her recliner, Maureen grinned like a mischievous schoolgirl who had just discovered the headmistress's gin. "Told you," she said. "They get the dramatics from you."

I almost dropped my mug. Not because she was here—she'd been "here" for days now—but because she looked vivid today. The light in the room had caught the edges of her hair, that reddish colour I could never describe without sounding lovesick and inaccurate.

The Georgia Tech jumper I was wearing (it is blue, not white and gold, or gold and white—yes, yes, everyone who ever went to Georgia Tech, hold your emails; it is blue in my memory and that's the version that bought me a life) hummed against my skin like a barely tuned radio.

Claire clapped her hands once. "Dad. Tell us again how you met Mum."

Sophie's face softened a little. Daniel shifted forward. They all knew the story, but they were my kids—they loved the hits. Give them the greatest track on my life's album.

"All right," I said, settling back. "But if I get to the bridge, someone's making me another coffee."

I cleared my throat.

It was the summer I'd told everyone I was going to be an architect, because at that age you announced careers like weather forecasts: largely optimistic, occasionally accurate, and based on cloud formations you didn't understand. I had landed in Atlanta in 1962, with the arrogance of a 19-year-old, and an unholy love for a yellow insect in a sweater—Buzz, the Georgia Tech mascot. I'd wanted to go to Georgia Tech, design magnificent buildings, and own more pencils than any man should.

"And I loved the entire vibe. The Ramblin' Wreck, the songs, the idea of being a Ramblin' Wreck myself—which now, as your father, I can confirm I did not achieve my goal and went into banking instead."

"Confirmed," Daniel said.

"So, I'm wandering around the campus store, right? This place was like a shrine to school spirit. Flags. Banners. Mugs with handles large enough for a handshake. There were rows of jumpers—sweaters, for those who track such differences— with little patches and big letters and the promise that if you bought one, you'd become the person whose teeth gleamed in yearbook photos."

Maureen coughed delicately. "Get to the part where I appear like an angel with a sales quota."

"And then," I said, "a young woman walked up to me. She had reddish hair—"

Sophie sighed. "We know. Like a fox fell into a sunbeam."

"Like autumn whispered a secret," I corrected because accuracy mattered. "She smiled at me, and you know how people say a smile lights up the room? This was the entire building. The power grid dimmed for a second. She said, 'Can I help you?' and I tried to speak, but what came out was a noise only dogs and shy librarians hear."

"I would have paid to see that," Daniel said.

"She introduced herself—'I'm Maureen'—and I thought, *Good Lord, the sales staff are using mind-control names now.* It floated like music. I pointed at a shelf of jumpers and said, in an accent that was only ninety percent Cuban (on my parents side) and ten percent terror (all mine), 'The blue, perhaps?'"

"Blue? You know that's not the colours of Georgia Tech? The colours are gold and white. This one is just an imitation. Not a genuine Georgia Tech apparel." Claire said, side-eyeing Sophie and nodding towards me.

"Yes, I know, but I wanted a blue jumper," I said. "A beautiful blue Georgia Tech jumper with the school's name across the front. She plucked it from a rack in the back of the shop like a magician pulling a rabbit and held it up to me, eyes narrowing. She was calculating everything from my size, to my innocence and credit limit. I looked at the price tag and because it was not 'genuine' it fitted my budget just right and I even had something left for lunch. So I nodded, looked back at her and she smiled. I swear I heard a choir sing so I got the jumper. And I bought the hope that came with it."

Maureen curled her lip. "You also bought a keychain you pretended was for 'a friend.'"

That keychain still opens the mailbox I don't own, I thought, barely holding myself from saying it aloud.

"And then?" Sophie prompted.

"And then," I said, heart thumping at the memory even now, "I don't entirely remember how I formed the sentence, but I asked her if she'd have coffee with me. I expected laughter, or a pamphlet about customer relations, but she said yes. Just like that. She said yes, and we agreed to meet, and everything after that is… well, your lives, frankly."

For a moment, silence settled like a soft blanket. I saw them remembering their mum: the way she'd tilt her head when you lied, the way she could listen with her entire face, the way she could find the funniest line through the worst problem. I glanced at the armchair. She was watching them—tender, proud and delighted.

"So, Mum, an Aussie, was working at the American shop. Did not you find it strange, Dad?"

"No, we had a lot of folks from other parts of the world at the university, and later I found out her dad was a visiting professor of engineering from the University of Technology in New South Wales doing a sting at Georgia Tech, and she was working on her own degree too. A Bachelor of Science in Music Technology. Imagine that. At Georgia Tech!"

"Yes," said Sophie, "and we know how well Mum sang, right?"

We all chuckled at that while Maureen gave me the look.

"Okay," Claire said, clearing her throat. "Thank you for the story, Dad. And for the repeated insistence that blue is a Georgia Tech colour."

"Historically contentious," Daniel muttered.

"But," Claire continued, businesslike again, "we didn't call this meeting just for the nostalgia. We're worried."

"About what?" I asked, though I knew.

Sophie lifted her phone like a court exhibit. "About you and what you told Daniel last week on the phone. That you were, well, seeing Mum."

"I am," I said. "Seeing her."

"Dad." Claire's voice softened, but the words themselves were ironed. "We all miss Mum. We talk to her sometimes too. But you've been different."

"How?" I asked.

"You leave out two mugs now," Daniel said, pointedly looking at the mug next to my recliner and the other next to Maureen's.

"You've been laughing alone," Sophie said, clearly talking about yesterday morning when she'd walked out the back to see me laughing alone with the plants. Of course, I hadn't been alone, but no one else could see Maureen scolding the coleus for invading the ixora's pot.

"You've been happier," Claire finished with suspicion, as if happiness itself had forged her signature and she was out for her comeuppance.

From the recliner, Maureen popped her cheeks like a kid trying to whistle. "Tell them I'm wearing the acceptable version of my hair." "I can't," I hissed. "You know this is going to make me look insane."

"You do that fine on your own," she said, winking.

"See, Dad, you are doing it again," chimed in Claire.

I set my coffee down. "All right," I said. "You all asked me to be honest, yes? So, here's honest: your mother is here almost every day."

They stared at me as if I had just admitted to keeping bees in the kitchen.

"Here. Where?" Daniel asked finally.

I gestured to the recliner. "There."

They turned. Looked at the very empty piece of furniture. Looked back at me.

"Oh my God," Claire said. "He's talking to furniture."

"Rude," Maureen said, crossing her legs, which I swear made the cushion indent. "I'm very *high-end* furniture."

Sophie tapped her phone with frantic grace. "Early signs of dementia," she whispered to herself. "Hallucinations. Paranoia. Increased crushes on upholstery."

"I'm not hallucinating," I said.

"Dad," Claire said, "I love you. We love you. But Mum is gone."

I felt a familiar ache; the kind that climbed my ribs like ivy and settled into my bones like a boa constrictor preparing dinner. "She is," I said. "And she isn't."

"Which is it?" Daniel asked gently.

I tugged at the collar of the jumper. "Both."

Claire rubbed her temples. "Dad, you're wearing that old college Georgia Tech jumper again. You've been wearing it every day."

"Because it's comfortable," I lied. "Also, when I first put it on, Maureen popped into the room like a radio station finding signal at dusk. So I keep wearing it to keep seeing her."

"It's a thousand degrees," Sophie said. "You're basically slow-cooking."

Maureen snorted. "They have a point."

"Here's the thing," I said. "When I wear this, I can see her. Hear her. We talk."

"You talk?" Claire asked.

"Yes."

"About what?" Sophie asked, sceptical and curious at once—the family default setting.

I shrugged. "Everything. Coffee. The backyard, the front yard, the plants. Daniel still hasn't fixed the dripping tap. She called Claire 'Madam Prime Minister' yesterday and then laughed at her own joke for five minutes. She told Sophie to moisturise her knees."

Sophie's eyes widened. "Mum absolutely would say that."

"She would," Claire whispered.

"Make him prove it," Daniel said, though he didn't sound convinced of anything except his wish to go home.

"Prove it how?" I asked.

"I don't know," he said. "Ask her a question only Mum would know."

Maureen perked up. "Ooooh. Quiz night."

"Okay, back in 2022, which one of you hid the last slice of lemon cake in the washing machine?" I said promptly.

All three of them blushed which was encouraging.

"Fine," Claire said. "We all did that once."

"Twice," Maureen corrected. "And Sophie left the plate in there."

Therefore, I repeated Maureen's answer to them.

"Okay, that is hauntingly accurate," Sophie said, lowering her phone.

Daniel leaned forward, elbows on knees. "Dad, maybe you're remembering her so well that it feels like she's here. I mean you knew her so well, and you spent so much of your lives together…" He looked at the empty chair, then away. "I talk to her too. In my car. I ask her about the traffic."

"She always knows," Maureen said. "Tell him it's the red sedan that blocks the roundabout on Warwick."

"She says it's the red sedan that blocks the roundabout on Warwick," I repeated. "Every day."

Daniel's mouth fell open. "That… okay, that is not… that's probably true for statistical reasons."

Claire stood.

Pacing now.

"We're not trying to bully you out of your feelings, Dad. We just want to make sure you're okay. That you're not stuck."

I looked at Maureen. She tilted her head at me, eyes bright. "Tell them," she said. "Tell them the truth like we always have."

I sighed. "I am stuck," I said before quickly rushing to add, "And moving. Both. Like one of those puzzles where you slide tiles around until a picture appears. I don't know what the full picture is yet. But when I wear this–" I plucked at the jumper, "–I get to have a cup of coffee with your mother. And if that makes me mad, then so be it. I have survived worse things than being thought mad. Like the era when Daniel was into interpretive dance."

"Hey," Daniel said, though he grinned.

Sophie's phone buzzed.

She ignored it.

"If Mum is here," she said, voice small, "what does she think about us?"

Maureen's face softened like butter on warm toast. "Oh, honey," she said. "Everything."

I pulled my youngest daughter closer, wrapping my arm around her. "She thinks Claire is still trying to manage the sun," I said, repeating Maureen's words as they left her ghostly lips. "And that she might, just once, let it set without a spreadsheet. She thinks Daniel is kinder than he knows and that he should call that lovely lady from the bookshop in the Narellan shopping centre. And she thinks Sophie has a brilliant brain that should occasionally sleep."

Sophie swallowed. Claire stopped pacing. Daniel coughed into his fist.

"And about you?" Claire asked. "What does she think about you, Dad?"

I looked at Maureen.

She rolled her eyes fondly. "Tell her I think you're an idiot who should drink more water and stop watching TV in that position where your neck looks like a question mark."

"She thinks I should drink more water," I translated with a smile. "And stop watching TV in that position where my neck looks like a question mark."

Sophie blinked rapidly. Daniel studied the carpet. Claire exhaled.

"Okay," Claire said finally. "Okay. I can see how this helps you. But, Dad, we're still worried. Because—you're wearing a jumper like armour. And if people see you talking to a recliner, we're going to have to have a second family meeting in a public place with soft lighting and a professional present."

"Therapist," Maureen said. "She means therapist."

"I know what she means," I said back to Maureen, which made the kids nervous.

"Maybe," Daniel offered, "we could be here sometimes? Join for coffee or a meal?"

"We can," Sophie said. "But ground rules. No swapping my moisturiser."

Maureen nods.

"Your mother agrees," I said.

Claire sat again. "All right, then. Next step." She squared herself off at me. "Take off the jumper."

Maureen's eyes went wide. "Oh no," she said. "Here comes the magic trick."

I hesitated.

The room shrank in anticipation.

My hands found the hem. Claire's face was firm. Daniel's was resigned. Sophie held her phone like a rosary.

I pulled the jumper over my head.

The room's air changed, like someone had opened a window in a memory. The recliner was suddenly just fabric and stuffing and a dent that could be anybody's. It was like standing on a pier after the boat had slipped away. I kept my face neutral, as if neutrality could protect me from the very particular cold of absence.

"Well?" Claire asked, eyes darting to the chair.

"Is Mum still here?" Sophie whispered.

I stared at the chair, at the space Maureen had occupied with a vibrant, inconvenient joy. "No," I said evenly. "She went to check on the red sedan."

Sophie's mouth twisted. "Dad."

"Fine." I folded the jumper in my lap, ridiculous as a toddler with a blanket. "No."

Claire tried to keep the triumph off her face and almost succeeded. "So, you see, Dad," she said gently. "This is a thing you're doing. A coping mechanism."

"An enchanted garment," Daniel said. "Like The Sisterhood of the Travelling Pants, but for bereaved men and college merchandise."

"It just helps," I said.

"We understand," Claire said, and for a moment she truly did.

Then she stood, switched back into practical mode. "Okay. New plan. Wear the jumper at home. Not in public. Hydrate. We'll do dinner once a month, rotating around our places, and someone will come over to bully you about laundry."

"Lovely," I said. "I've always wanted to live in a supportive dictatorship."

"We love you," Sophie said, surprisingly fierce, sliding onto the arm of my chair. "Even if you're dating knitwear."

I laughed. It turned into something else for a heartbeat. "I love you too."

They gathered their things.

Claire snapped a photo of the "to be filed" stack on my coffee table, then assured me she'd turn it into a workflow, which was a thing only she knew how to make. Daniel promised to fix the tap. Sophie threatened to confiscate my remote if I didn't text by nine.

At the door, Claire paused. "If you see her," she said, gaze carefully neutral, "tell her we're okay."

"I will," I said.

"And tell her," Daniel added, pretending to adjust his sleeve, "that I didn't cry at the ad about the labrador and the postal worker."

"I will lie convincingly," I said.

Sophie leaned in, whispered, "Tell her I moisturised."

"Will do."

They left in a flurry of keys and adult competence.

The house settled again.

I sat there with the jumper folded in my lap like a faithful dog.

"Well," I said to the quiet room.

From everywhere and nowhere, a laugh answered. I pulled the jumper back on. There she was in the recliner, smirking, eyes glossy, the familiar, impossible joy of her.

"They're convinced you've lost your marbles," she said.

"Have I?" I asked.

"Probably," she said. "But you misplace everything, eventually."

"Thanks."

She tilted her head. "They're good kids."

"The best," I said. "Even when they stage coups."

She took me in, the whole of me. "You were handsome," she said, apropos of nothing. "In that college store. Trying to look like you belonged anywhere. You always belonged with me, you know."

"Say that again," I said, because I was greedy.

"You. Belonged. With me," she intoned, as if reciting the recipe for the only cake that ever mattered.

I breathed. The jumper was warm. The tea had gone cold. A miracle occupied the recliner only I could see.

I raised my coffee mug as if it were full. "To the Ramblin' Wreck, to coffee, tea, to worried children, to money I didn't have, and to a blue jumper that bought me a life."

Maureen saluted with an invisible mug.

"And to you," she said. "My lovely idiot. My architect of nonsense. My man."

"For how long?" I asked suddenly, not ready for the answer but needing to ask anyway.

"For as long as it helps," she said. "And then for the rest of your life, but in a unique room."

Together we sat there—the living and the loved, the visible and the true—in a silence that felt like home.

In the far off distance, I was sure I heard a car idling, red and guilty, at the Warwick roundabout. In here, my heart beat out the old rhythm—yes, yes, yes—as I met her eyes.

I stared at the recliner because I could. I stared at the jumper because I didn't know how not to.

I thought of Claire's spreadsheets, Daniel's kind hands, Sophie's anxious thumbs. I thought of a store, a smile, and a man who fell in love while pretending to shop.

"You know," Maureen said after a while, "you *are* talking to furniture."

"I'm talking to you," I said.

She laughed. "Same thing, sometimes."

We sat there a while longer, not needing to say more.

Eventually, the coffee demanded mercy. I stood, joints narrating their protests, and carried the mug to the kitchen.

From the lounge, Maureen called, "And don't forget to drink water!"

I turned back, grinning like a fool. "Yes, dear."

Her voice softened. "Tell them I'm here."

"I did," I said.

And maybe that was the lesson wedged between the silly, sacred folds of this jumper: that grief is a story we tell together. Sometimes a story with spreadsheets and symptom checklists, sometimes with jokes about upholstery, sometimes with the quiet clink of a mug in an empty room that wasn't empty at all.

As I filled the glass at the sink, I heard laughter again, hers and mine stitched together across the years like the letters on my chest. I drank. I lived. I went back to the lounge and sat down with my love, who was here and not, exactly as she needed to be until I learned to be otherwise.

And if my children thought I'd lost my marbles—well, marbles were only useful when you played. And by all that existed in heaven, I intended to keep playing.

THE FITTED-SHEET CHALLENGE

It had been a week since Maureen had come back into my life, or rather, back into my laundry room, kitchen, lounge, and pretty much every corner of this house. And I had to admit— I was having the best time I'd had in weeks.

Who knew the afterlife came with a side hustle as a home management consultant? Every day she found something I was doing wrong—or not doing at all—and gave me pointers.

Yesterday, she showed me how to stack the dishwasher without looking like I'd just dumped a box of Lego pieces inside. The day before that, she walked me through the correct way to fold a T-shirt without ending up with a lopsided origami project. Today, though, today was a whole different battlefield: the fitted sheet.

Now, I'd been alive long enough to raise kids, pay taxes, and learn to navigate IKEA instructions (barely), but I still hadn't cracked the code of folding a fitted sheet. My lifelong method was balling it up like some laundry-based meteor and shoving it into the linen cupboard until the door wouldn't close anymore. Maureen was not having it.

"Josh," she said in that calm, patient tone that told me she knew this was going to be ugly, "if you can do this, you can do anything."

She might as well have been prepping me to defuse a bomb.

I was standing in the laundry room, sheet in my hands, corners flopping around like a rebellious squid. Maureen, hovering beside me in her soft glow, looked perfectly composed, as if this were the moment she had been waiting for.

"First, hold it lengthwise," she instructed.

"Lengthwise?" I asked. "It's a square!"

"Rectangle," she corrected, with the authority that only a wife could have. "Now, find two corners. Put one inside the other."

I stared at the elastic edges. "They all look like corners. It's a trap."

"Josh…" Her voice softened like it always did when she knew I was two seconds from quitting. "Watch me."

She made the motion with her hands—ghost hands—and for a second; I swear the sheet seemed to fold itself gracefully in her direction. I tried to mimic it.

My result looked more like I was wrestling a manta ray.

"Okay," I said, blowing out a frustrated breath. "Maybe if I just—"

"No," she interrupted firmly. "You can't just crumple it. We are folding, not surrendering."

That was when I had my great idea. I marched out of the room, leaving the sheet sprawled on the floor like a casualty of war, and came back with my laptop.

"YouTube," I declared triumphantly. "Surely, in the vast universe of the internet, someone has unlocked the secret."

Maureen folded her ghostly arms and raised an eyebrow. "You're going to let a stranger in a video teach you instead of me?"

"Yes," I said without hesitation. "Because at least they'll let me pause them."

She rolled her eyes but leaned in as I typed "how to fold a fitted sheet" into the search bar. Thousands of results. I clicked the first one, and a cheerful woman on the screen greeted me like she was about to save my soul.

"Step one," the woman said. "Hold the sheet lengthwise."

I froze, glaring at the laptop, then at Maureen. "See? Even she's in on it. Lengthwise! How am I supposed to know what that means?"

Maureen laughed, that light laugh I had missed so much, and came closer. "Just try again. You've got this."

So, I did.

I pinched two corners, tried to tuck one inside the other, and—miracle of miracles—it actually worked. For about three seconds. Then the elastic snapped out of place, and the whole thing collapsed like a circus tent in a storm.

"ARGH!" I shouted, throwing my arms up. "This sheet is possessed."

"You're possessed," Maureen whispered. "By impatience."

Her voice wasn't scolding, though.

It was soft, coaxing, the way she used to talk to me when I was on the edge of giving up on something. And she repeated it: "If you can do this, you can do anything."

I sighed, bent down, and picked the sheet back up.

And somehow, between her hovering guidance and the YouTube lady's relentless optimism, I did manage to fold the thing. It wasn't pretty. It wasn't symmetrical. It wasn't even particularly flat. But it was folded.

Maureen beamed at me like I'd just earned a PhD in domestic miracles.

After the triumph of finally folding that damned fitted sheet, the rest of the laundry should've felt just as easy. Sheets. Towels. Pillowcases. Fold, stack, repeat.

I was almost proud of myself—almost convinced I was getting the hang of this whole domestic survival nonsense.

Then I reached for the Georgia Tech jumper.

"Josh?" Maureen's voice drifted toward me—soft, cautious, like she already knew what was coming.

"I'm just… washing it," I said, though the words didn't feel steady in my mouth.

And the moment I took it off, she faded from the room. Not dramatically, not suddenly—just… gone.

Maybe I had done it without thinking.

Maybe the universe nudged it forward like, *Here, mate, time to feel something you've been avoiding.*

Or maybe grief is a boomerang—you throw it somewhere dark, and it always circles back, waiting to smack you in the chest when you least expect it.

I held the jumper for a long time, tracing the faded letters with my thumb.

GEORGIA TECH.

My second skin now so I can be with her.

And as I stood there, the familiar tightness gathered in my throat.

Ridiculous, I told myself.

Absolutely ridiculous.

I forced myself to move.

I placed it gently into the washing machine, added detergent, and told myself it was fine.

Normal steps.

Ordinary steps.

Just laundry.

Then I pressed Start.

The drum began to spin, and the jumper disappeared into the whirl of water and fabric.

That was the moment something cracked inside me.

Maybe it was the sound of the machine.

Maybe it was seeing the jumper tossed around, slipping out of view like she had slipped out of my life.

Maybe it was the quiet enormity of the moment—doing something and she was not here with me.

I gripped the edge of the machine, knuckles white, and tried to breathe.

I couldn't.

The sob punched its way out of me before I had a chance to stop it—a sharp, helpless sound that felt like a rib snapping from the inside.

"I don't—" I choked on the words, swallowing hard. "I don't know why I'm crying."

I wiped my face with my sleeve, but the tears kept streaming, big ones.

The kind that shake your whole frame, make you feel like the earth has split under your feet.

"It's just a jumper," I whispered, even though we both knew it wasn't.

Not even close.

"It's stupid. God, I'm being stupid."

I looked at the machine—at the spinning, churning circle—and the grief rose again, raw and wordless.

"This is all I have left to hold," I whispered.

"When you were here… you were *here*. And now I'm crying in a laundry room over a jumper because… because it's the closest thing I have to you."

Saying it gutted me.

Split me open like a seam I'd been pretending wasn't frayed.

But letting the words out—letting them fall into the open space between us—felt like unclenching a fist I didn't realise I'd kept shut for months.

The machine spun, the jumper tumbled and then the machine stopped.

I opened the lid, took the soaking wet jumper and put it on.

Maureen did not reappear.

"Maybe the jumper does not work when wet," I almost laugh to myself and then I place my forehead on my arm and my breath trembled.

And finally, I let it come—the grief I'd been holding back, the ache I'd been pretending was manageable.

And I stood there, soaking wet wearing the jumper and clutching cold metal, crying for no reason and for every reason.

Because love leaves echoes.

I know that now in a way I never understood before—echoes that settle into the quiet corners of a house, into the fabric of routines, into the very texture of a jumper you wear. They reverberate long after the person who made the echoes is gone. I can still feel her when I wear it and the faint scent of her that refuses to fade, like love finding any excuse to linger.

Because loss hollows you out.

Not all at once, not dramatically, but slowly, spoonful by spoonful, until you realise you've been walking around with spaces inside you where she used to live. And it only takes something small, something gentle, to touch those hollowed places and make them ring again.

Because sometimes the smallest, softest thing like a worn blue jumper, faded at the sleeves, stretched at the collar, loved far beyond its years becomes a doorway.

A doorway into everything you still miss: her warmth, her laugh, the way she tucked herself into me when she was cold, the way she'd curl up beside me on the couch and rest her head against my shoulder.

That jumper holds entire winters of our life together.

Maybe more.

And standing there with it in my hands—my thumb tracing the letters I realise something painful and oddly tender: I needed to wash it.

Not to erase her, not to silence the echo, but because caring for it feels like caring for her.

Like keeping her close in the only way I can now.

So I placed it gently into the washing machine, as though it were something fragile, something sacred, which, in a way, it is.

And when the drum stopped spinning I wore it again.

Soaked and wet.

Because maybe that's what love asks of you after loss, not to be strong, not to move on, not to pretend the hollow spaces don't exist.

But to show up anyway.

To care for what remains.

To let yourself cry over a jumper because it means she mattered.

Still matters.

Because love doesn't disappear.

It changes shape.

And sometimes it looks exactly like a man standing in a laundry room, crying while wearing a soaked and wet worn blue jumper as he carries every echo of the woman he still loves.

THERAPY OR EXORCISM

The phone rang just after dinner. I should've known by the way her "Hi, Dad" sounded—sweet but loaded—that this wasn't a casual check-in.

When your grown kids staged a family coup, you had little to no chance of fighting them off.

Especially when the ringleader is Claire, I thought. My eldest had inherited all her mother's determination and none of my ability to dodge confrontation.

"Dad," she said, "we've been talking."

"Ah," I said, bracing myself immediately. "Nothing good ever comes after those words."

"You need grief counselling."

There it was.

I tried the classic stall. "Counselling? Well, I mean, I've been counselling myself pretty well lately. Just this week, I folded a fitted sheet. That's progress."

"Dad."

"When a man folds elastic corners without crying, that's healing."

"Dad!" Her tone shut me up.

Claire had mastered the mother-in-training voice years ago.

She softened. "We're worried about you. You need someone professional. Someone who isn't us."

I muttered something about professionals costing money and about already having Maureen as my unpaid life coach–thankfully, I didn't say the last part aloud.

By the end of the call, I was "volunteered."

My daughters had booked the appointment.

All I had to do was show up.

So that's how I shuffled into a therapist's office on a Thursday morning, wearing my Georgia Tech jumper as armour but with no Maureen in sight.

What is she waiting for? I thought.

Call it superstition, call it a security blanket, but if Maureen came and went with this thing, I wasn't taking chances.

The waiting room smelled faintly of peppermint tea and anxiety. The magazines were six months old. I resisted the urge to make a break for the exit, but before I could, a door opened.

"Josh?" A kind-faced woman in her 50s smiled at me. "Come on in."

I trudged behind her into an office decorated in soothing beige. The couch looked too clean to sit on. I sat anyway.

And then, of course, Maureen appeared.

Perched right on the armrest like a queen on her throne, she glowed faintly in the daylight. She leaned close to my ear.

"Tell her you cry when you see toothpaste commercials."

"Not helpful," I whispered.

The therapist tilted her head. "Sorry?"

"Uh, nothing. Clearing my throat."

She smiled kindly and opened her notebook. "Why don't you tell me why you're here?"

"Well," I began, clasping my hands. "My kids think I need grief counselling."

"They love you very much," she said warmly.

"Or they're tired of me calling them whenever I can't figure out the Netflix remote," I muttered.

"Both," Maureen whispered. "Definitely both."

I pressed on. "Anyway, my wife, Maureen, passed away, and it's been hard."

The therapist nodded sympathetically. "And how do you cope with the difficult moments?"

Before I could answer, Maureen piped up again. "Don't mention how you sing in the shower. That's too pathetic."

I clenched my jaw. "Sometimes I walk. Or talk to her picture."

"Good," the therapist said, jotting notes.

"Or complain to the radio," I added before I could stop myself.

Her pen froze. "Complain to the radio?"

"Uh, long story. It doesn't matter."

Maureen giggled. "Tell her you threaten to throw them out when they play Lionel Richie."

I snorted and then tried to disguise it as a cough.

The therapist leaned in. "It's okay to laugh. Laughter is healthy."

That only made it worse.

Maureen, egging me on, whispered: "Say you burst into tears at the pet food aisle because snack bags remind you of me."

I lost it.

Out of nowhere, I barked a laugh loud enough to startle myself.

The therapist's eyes lit up. "That's wonderful! That release. You're letting yourself feel."

"Oh, I'm feeling alright," I muttered.

She clasped her hands together. "Tell me more about this breakthrough."

Maureen smirked, leaning so close I could feel the chill of her not-quite-breath. "Go on, my Cuban lover boy. Tell her your dead wife is heckling you during this session."

I choked back another laugh. "It's just that grief sneaks up in funny ways, you know?"

The therapist nodded. "Yes, humour is often a mask for pain. But I think you're processing remarkably well."

Processing. If only she knew.

We went on like this for nearly an hour.

Every time the therapist asked a serious question, Maureen delivered running commentary:

"Say you smell my perfume in the laundry aisle."

"Tell her you're too stubborn to buy new socks."

"Admit you still don't know how to work the oven timer."

It was impossible not to grin.

Which the therapist, bless her heart, interpreted as resilience.

By the end, she leaned back in her chair, clearly pleased. "Josh, I think you're on the right track. You've accepted your loss, you're laughing again, and you're here. That's progress."

"Really?" I asked, feeling like a fraud.

"Really. I'd like to see you again, but honestly, you're doing well."

Maureen raised her ghostly eyebrows. "Well, at least you're paying someone to ignore me now."

I bit the inside of my cheek to stop from laughing again.

The therapist handed me a card with her number. I thanked her politely, shuffled out, and only once we were in the parking lot did, I let the laughter spill.

Maureen was right beside me, glowing brighter in the morning sun.

"You were terrible in there," I told her.

"You were worse," she said with a grin. "But hey, gold star for not telling her about your shower concerts."

I shook my head. "One day, you're going to get me committed."

"Too late," she teased. "Our kids already think you' re nuts."

I stopped at my car, slid inside and, for the first time in months, felt something close to lightness. Not because of therapy or imaginary breakthroughs, but because even here, in the most serious of places, Maureen was still Maureen.

And maybe that was the best grief counselling I could ever get and enjoy.

FIRST FIGHT

I'll admit it: I was riding high. Not Everest high, but at least Mount Kosciuszko high. After all, I'd stared down the beast known as the fitted sheet and come out the other side with something that at least resembled a folded rectangle.

It was wrinkled, lumpy, and vaguely threatening, but it was folded.

And once you've survived that ordeal, you strut around the house like a man who's unlocked life's secrets.

So, there I was, chest puffed out, feeling like I'd finally figured out this "living alone" thing.

Chores? Pfft.

I had a system.

Laundry?

Piled in the machine with one pod of detergent—maybe two, depending on how generous I was feeling.

Vacuuming?

I'd gotten very good at kicking crumbs under the couch.

But the crown jewel of my domestic confidence?

The dishwasher.

Yes, that gleaming silver box in the kitchen that Maureen had dragged me to Harvey Norman to buy. "It has a ten-year warranty, Josh," she had said. "We'll probably die before it does."

Well, she hadn't been entirely wrong.

Anyway, I thought I'd mastered it.

Plates leaned, coffee mugs stacked, spoons spooned. I even ran the 'eco' cycle sometimes just to feel virtuous.

Until Maureen intervened.

I'd just closed the door on a creative load—art, really, a mosaic of ceramic and steel—when I felt that familiar chill and saw her perched on the counter, arms crossed, glowing faintly in the kitchen light.

"What," I said, feeling oddly defensive, "is that look for?"

"That," she said, "is the look of a woman watching her husband commit crimes against kitchenware."

"Crimes?" I scoffed. "I call it innovation! Look at this arrangement! I've maximised the cubic capacity."

She floated down and peered inside.

"You've blocked the spray arm with a soup ladle. Nothing on the top rack is going to get clean."

"Yes, it will," I argued. Why was she arguing with me on this? I knew what I was doing! "Water is sneaky. It'll find its way around."

Her eyes narrowed. "This is why our plates always had mysterious specks. You've been loading it wrong this whole time."

"Wrong?" I threw my hands up. "Maureen, you're dead. You don't need sparkling dishes anymore!"

The words were out before I could stop them.

The kitchen went silent, except for the hum of the fridge.

She gasped theatrically, pressing a hand to her ghostly chest. "How dare you? Death does not diminish my standards, Joshua."

I groaned. "Don't use my full name."

She pointed an accusing finger. "Plates go on the bottom rack, facing inward. Mugs and glasses on top. Utensils separated: forks here, knives there, spoons not piled in like they're cuddling."

I snorted. "Separated? What are they, middle schoolers at a dance?"

Her glow brightened dangerously. "Josh, I taught you better."

"Correction," I said, grabbing a plate and waving it like a white flag, "you tried to teach me better. I resisted. And I shall resist again!"

Maureen gasped, clutching her ghostly pearls. "This is mutiny in my kitchen!"

"It's my kitchen now," I declared, spinning the plate dramatically.

"Not while you're loading it like a caveman!"

"Cavemen didn't have dishwashers!"

"They'd have done it better than this!"

By now, I was practically shouting at the open dishwasher. She was hovering above it like a furious general, barking orders. I was countering with every ounce of stubbornness I had. The absurdity didn't register until I heard a voice behind me.

"Dad?"

I froze.

Slowly, I turned.

And there stood Sophie. Her eyes were wide, her mouth open so wide a Ford truck could have parked in it, and in that moment, I knew. I was caught.

She looked at me, then at the dishwasher, then back at me. "Are you yelling at the plates or are you talking to mum?"

I scrambled. "Uh, I am speaking with your mother, honey."

"What?"

"Speaking to your mum. You know I said that is what I do now. It helps." I blurted. "

Sophie blinked.

Behind me, Maureen just watches us.

Sophie's expression softened into something worse than suspicion—pity. "Dad, please stop. This is heartbreaking."

My shoulders sagged.

I muttered something I do not even remember what it is now, but the damage was done. Sophie stepped forward, gently closing the dishwasher door as if she were putting a lid on my madness.

"I'm calling Claire and Daniel," she said firmly.

"No! No need for that. You know I do this. I told Daniel…"

"Dad…" Her voice cracked a little.

"We just want you to be okay."

I felt my ears burning.

My daughter thought I was losing it, all of them were, and maybe she wasn't wrong. After all, from her perspective, I was shouting at plates, arguing with an appliance. She couldn't see my ghost wife standing by the counter, wiping ghost tears sometimes.

Sophie gave me a long hug—one of those careful hugs people give to someone they're afraid might shatter—and left the house.

As soon as the door closed, Maureen said: "Oh, Josh, you should've seen your face!"

"I know," I grumbled. "She thinks I'm ready for the looney house."

"Well, you waved a plate around like you were declaring independence."

I shot her a glare. "You were egging me on!"

"And you rose to the occasion!" She dissolved into laughter again. "Oh, I haven't had this much fun since—well, since the last time you tried to assemble IKEA furniture, but I am sorry that Sophie got so upset."

I slumped into a chair, rubbing my temples. "I know Maureen, this is just great. Now our kids are going to hold an intervention. Maybe they'll ship me off to one of those places with crocheted blankets and pudding cups."

"Could be worse," she said. "At least you'll finally have people who appreciate your dishwasher technique."

I groaned. "sometimes you enjoy this too much."

"Of course, I do. You're adorable when you're flustered."

I picked up the abandoned plate, turning it over in my hands.

"You Maureen, Sophie looked at me as if I were broken."

Maureen's voice softened.

"She's just worried. They all are. They can't see me, Josh. To them, it's just you in here. Alone, shouting at dishes."

I swallowed hard.

"I know Maureen, but I did tell them I see you even though they cannot. I am not sure they believe me so maybe they are right, maybe I am losing it."

"You're not," she said firmly, perching on the table. "You're grieving. And you're stubborn. And yes, you're a little ridiculous. But you're not crazy."

I gave her a sideways glance.

"Says my ghost wife in the kitchen where I just told our daughter that I'm okay because all I am doing is just talking to her dead mum."

She grinned. "Exactly. Who better to judge?"

"We just had our first fight, right?" I spoke. "Since…"

"Yes, darling, we did. One of the many—what did you call them? Oh yes—'discussions' we had over the 25 years we had together."

"Yeah. Always silly ones at that. Right?"

Maureen looked at me and just smiled.

Despite myself, I smiled back and laughed. A tired, embarrassed laugh, but real.

Maureen floated closer, brushing her ghostly hand near mine. "Now, how about we reload that dishwasher properly before your ten-year warranty gets revoked from the afterlife?"

I groaned again but picked up another plate.

And if Sophie had peeked just then, she would've seen her father carefully, almost reverently, lining up dishes in perfect rows.

Arguing under his breath with no one she could see.

SLIPUP

Going to therapy without my Georgia Tech jumper felt like walking into battle without armour. But dry-cleaning waits for no man, even one haunted by his wife.

There I was, session number two, perched on the therapist's cream-coloured couch, feeling naked without my security blanket. She gave me the same warm smile as last time—the smile that said, 'Don't worry, you're safe here', which was exactly what made me want to bolt.

"How have you been since our last session, Josh?" she asked, pen poised.

"Great," I said a little too quickly. "Really great. Busy. Productive."

"Tell me about that."

I launched into my new routine, proud as a kid showing off a macaroni necklace. "Well, I've been learning new things around the house. YouTube's been a big help. Did you know there are entire channels dedicated to folding laundry? Not that I watch them for fun or anything. Strictly educational."

She chuckled softly. "That sounds like a positive step."

"Very positive," I said, nodding too hard. "For instance, I've just about mastered the fitted sheet. That's a tricky beast. But Maureen helped—"

I froze.

The word had slipped out before my brain could grab it.

My mouth, that traitor, had just flung open the door I'd been carefully guarding.

The therapist's pen stopped. "Maureen?"

I scrambled. "Uh, YouTube. You know Maureen's Magic Laundry Hacks. It's a channel."

Her brow furrowed. "I see."

I laughed, the nervous kind that sounds like a man about to confess to robbing a bank. "Yeah, lots of channels out there. People with… many names. Could've been Maureen, could've been… Maurice."

She tilted her head. "Josh, you mentioned your wife's name just now."

My throat tightened.

I could imagine Maureen materialising on the armrest beside me, chin propped in her hand and smirking like a cat who'd pushed the vase off the table.

"Tell her I taught you everything. Especially how to survive without me." That was what she would have said had she been here.

I cleared my throat. "Slip of the tongue."

The therapist leaned forward slightly.

"But was it? You've mentioned you've been finding new ways to cope. Sometimes, in grief, people feel their loved one guiding them. Do you feel Maureen gives you advice?"

Maureen would have winked at me added: "Go on. Admit I'm your spiritual life coach."

My palms grew clammy.

"Well, uh, sure, in a way. I mean, anyone who's been married as long as we were, you would kind of, you know,

know what the other person would say. Like a little voice in your head, right?"

"That can be very healthy," she said thoughtfully, scribbling something. "As long as you understand it's your memory of her voice, not her voice itself."

"Of course," I said quickly, nodding. "Exactly. Memory. Purely cerebral. No actual whispering going on."

I remembered Maureen mocking my fitted-sheet folding. She'd love to have heard the therapist right now.

I grinned despite myself, then tried to cover it with a cough. The therapist raised an eyebrow.

"You seem amused."

"Just remembering," I said. "She had a way of making fun of me. Endearing, really. Like when I waved a sheet around like a flag of surrender."

"Waved a sheet?"

Oh, brilliant. Now I was painting myself as a lunatic soldier of the laundry wars.

I sat up straighter, adopting my most serious voice.

"What I mean is—I try to imagine what Maureen would say. Like a mental checklist. It helps me not to feel so alone in the house."

The therapist studied me for a moment, her pen tapping.

"That can be a comforting tool, yes. But sometimes, Josh, we need to make sure those inner dialogues don't prevent us from living fully in the present. Do you feel you're able to distinguish between memory and reality?"

"Oh, yes. Absolutely," I said, too fast again. "Crystal clear. Never any confusion. None whatsoever."

I could have sworn Maureen would have blown me a ghostly kiss, clearly delighted, had she been here.

The therapist nodded, though she didn't look fully convinced. "Alright. We'll monitor that, then. For now, it sounds like you're making progress."

I exhaled slowly.

Progress, she said.

She thought I was doing fine.

Meanwhile, I was sitting there wondering what else my ghost of a wife would have said had she been in on this session.

We wrapped up the session with the usual polite affirmations—"Keep up the good work" and "You're adapting well"— before I shuffled out, my shirt sticking uncomfortably to my back.

The second I hit the sidewalk, I muttered under my breath, "I've got to be more careful."

Because here was the thing: I didn't mind the therapist.

She was kind. She meant well.

But she wasn't the one folding laundry beside me, cracking jokes, filling the house with warmth again.

She wasn't the one who still made me laugh until my sides hurt, who reminded me I could still learn new tricks, even at my age.

That was Maureen.

And if I slipped too much in there, if I let the giddy grin creep across my face one too many times, the therapist might think I belonged in a padded room instead of a kitchen with a half-loaded dishwasher.

I made myself a vow right there on the footpath outside the office:

Control yourself, Josh.

Smile less.

Keep it vague.

Protect Maureen.

Although she might be gone, she was still here.

And I wasn't about to let a slipup, or anyone, take that away from me.

INTERVENTION – TAKE TWO

If there was one thing I'd learned about my kids, it was that when they got together, I was doomed.

Separately, I could handle them. Claire with her boss voice, Sophie with her puppy eyes, Daniel with his sarcasm.

But united?

That was an ambush.

And sure enough, on Sunday afternoon, there they were in my lounge room—lined up on the couch like a jury, leaving me, the accused, to sit in the lone recliner.

Claire cleared her throat first; that was never a good sign.

She had a stack of papers on her lap.

Pamphlets.

Glossy ones with stock photos of smiling seniors holding hands. I didn't need to see the titles to know where this was going.

"Dad," she began, "we've been talking—"

"Of course you have," I muttered.

"—and we think it's time to get you some additional support. Here."

She thrust the first pamphlet toward me.

Finding Hope: A Grief Support Group Near You.

I held it gingerly, as if it might bite. "Lovely. But I've already got support."

"From whom?" Sophie piped up. "You're alone most of the time."

I bit my tongue, because the correct answer—your mother—would not help my case.

Sophie leaned forward, her eyes full of worry. "Maybe I should move in for a while. Just to monitor you."

"Monitor? What am I, a volcano?" I quickly stated.

"Sometimes you erupt," she said seriously. "Like with the dishwasher, remember?"

Daniel snorted. "Forget moving in. I think Dad should just downsize. Smaller house, less stress. Plus, he won't need to argue with appliances."

I threw up my hands. "I am fine! Look at me. Dishes washed, sheets folded, even vacuum lines in the carpet!"

Maureen appeared on the arm of my chair, invisible to everyone but me, grinning like a cat. "Tell them you're fine because I still boss you around from the afterlife."

I shook my head slightly. "I'm just talking things through with your mother."

The kids exchanged glances. Oh, that did not land well.

Claire folded her arms. "Dad, we understand. You miss her. We do too. But you can't keep pretending she's here."

Behind me, Maureen leaned closer, whispering gleefully: "Tell them I enjoy haunting the bathroom!"

And I, idiot that I am, nearly repeated it. The words got as far as my tongue before I caught myself.

"I ha-ha-ha—haunt the, uh…horrible pollen season!" I blurted, then launched into a fake cough so violent I nearly toppled out of the chair.

The kids stared.

"Dad," Sophie said gently, "this is heartbreaking."

"You keep saying that, Sophie. I am okay."

Daniel muttered, "This is sitcom gold, is what it is."

Claire held up another pamphlet: *Moving Forward Together: Counselling for Families.* She looked me square in the eye. "Please. Just consider it."

I waved the glossy brochure like a white flag.

"Fine. I'll consider it. But I'm telling you, I'm not crazy."

When they finally left—after a round of extra-long hugs and promises to "check in more often"—I collapsed back into my recliner, exhaling so hard I felt deflated.

Maureen was practically rolling on the floor, laughing. "Oh, Josh, 'horrible pollen season'? You should take that act on the road."

I covered my face with both hands and started laughing too, the laughter that tips into tears before you can stop it. My chest shook, my eyes burned, and through it all, I could hear her voice, teasing and tender all at once.

"Congratulations," I muttered, wiping my face. "We're officially the craziest couple in town."

Maureen perched beside me, her glow softening, her eyes warm. "Darling, we always were."

And for once, I couldn't argue.

GROUP THERAPY

If you thought one-on-one therapy was awkward, try sitting in a circle of folding chairs with 10 strangers, each clutching tissues like they were part of the dress code.

Yes, Claire had gone and done it—booked me into a local grief support group. "It'll be good for you, Dad," she'd said, patting my hand like I was 87 years old, frail and feeble. "Just… share."

Share. Right.

Because nothing says 'good time' like opening up to a bunch of strangers who all look like they wandered out of a pharmaceutical ad for depression meds.

I shuffled into the community centre room, jumper firmly on this time—clean, pressed and smelling faintly of starch and ghost-wife approval. Chairs in a circle, fluorescent lights buzzing overhead. A woman with kind eyes and an I'm Here to Help smile introduced herself as Marlene, the facilitator.

"Welcome, everyone. Tonight, we're going to talk about coping strategies."

I was already calculating the odds of faking a heart attack to get out of this. Maureen couldn't sit next to me, so she perched on a desk off to the side as if it were her personal throne, glowing softly and looking far too entertained.

"Oh, this is going to be good," she hollered from across the room. "Say you cope by yelling at dishwashers."

I hissed, "Not now."

The man next to me—a big guy with a bushy moustache—gave me a sympathetic nod, mistaking my whisper for grief.

Marlene clapped her hands gently. "Who'd like to share first?"

Naturally, everyone stared at their laps.

"Josh?" she said sweetly, like she'd heard my fervent wishes and denied me. "You're new. Would you like to start?"

Of course. Me.

I cleared my throat. "Well, my wife, Maureen, passed away a few months ago. It's been hard. But I've been learning things. Around the house. Folding fitted sheets. Cooking. Vacuuming."

A woman across the circle dabbed at her eyes. "That's so brave."

"Brave?" Maureen scoffed from her perch. "You nearly strangled yourself with that sheet."

I bit the inside of my cheek to stop laughing.

Marlene addressed me again. "And what helps you through those difficult moments, Josh?"

"Oh boy," Maureen hollered to me. "Tell them I haunt the bathroom again. Go on, I dare you."

I almost said it—again—but caught myself.

"Uh… YouTube. Lots of YouTube."

Marlene smiled. "That's wonderful. Sometimes learning new skills is a way of honouring our loved ones."

"Yes!" I latched onto that like a lifeline. "Exactly. I am honouring her. She, uh, gives me tips. In my head."

"Tips?" Marlene asked, pen ready.

"Yes. Like when I'm loading the dishwasher, I imagine what she'd say. You know, 'Don't cram the spoons together,' things like that."

Maureen laughed aloud and smirked. "Tell them you also imagine me calling you a caveman."

I nearly choked.

The moustache guy patted my back. "Take your time, brother. Take your time."

Around the circle, people started nodding sympathetically, as if my laughter/cough meltdown was a raw display of grief. Marlene's eyes glistened.

"This is beautiful," she said softly. "You're keeping Maureen alive in the most important way—through memory."

"Memory," I echoed to myself, nodding vigorously. "Yep. Memory. Not actual bathroom haunting or anything."

Maureen snorted so loudly I was sure the desk rattled.

The group went around, each person sharing their coping tricks—journals, long walks, gardening. When it circled back to me, Marlene smiled. "Josh, would you like to add anything else?"

Maureen stood up and walked over to me and leaned in, whispering, "Tell them you sleep better because I hog the covers even from beyond the grave."

I pinched the bridge of my nose. "Uh, I cope by laughing. At myself. At memories. At, uh… fitted sheets."

The group chuckled politely. Even Marlene smiled. "Laughter is healing."

"See?" I whispered sideways, glaring at Maureen. "For once, she agrees with me."

The moustache guy gave me a thumbs-up.

By the end of the hour, I'd shared enough awkward anecdotes to convince everyone I was both a grieving widower and a walking sitcom. When Marlene wrapped up with a soft, "We're so glad you're here, Josh. We will see you next week. Maybe bring the family with you", I thought I might actually escape unscathed.

That is, until Sophie appeared in the doorway. She'd driven me—her idea of subtle 'monitoring.' She watched me wave goodbye to the group and then gave me that worried-puppy look.

"Dad? Are you okay?"

"Peachy," I said. "I just processed a lot of fitted sheets tonight."

She sighed. "I'll tell Claire you did well."

Maureen floated beside me as we walked out, her glow warm against the night air. "You were magnificent. Especially the coughing fit."

I barked a laugh, then swallowed it before Sophie could hear.

My daughter was already convinced I was a few plates short of a full dishwasher. I didn't need to make it worse

When we got to the car, I scowled at Maureen and muttered, "Well, congratulations. Again. We're officially the craziest couple in town."

Maureen slipped into the passenger seat, grinning. "Josh, we always were."

And I couldn't help but laugh and cry at the same time, buckling my seat belt while my ghost wife heckled me all the way home.

89

JOINING THE CIRCLE

I should've known better. Really, I should have.

It started with Claire.

"Dad," she said, waving her phone like it was a gavel, "Daniel and I are coming with you to your next grief group session. For support."

"For support? It's not a PTA meeting." I asked.

"It'll help," she said firmly.

Daniel grinned. "Besides, it'll be hilarious watching you cry over fitted sheets again."

And so, a week later, there we were: me, Claire, and Daniel, marching into the community centre like some sort of tragic sitcom family. Sophie had volunteered to drive but conveniently 'had plans,' which I suspected meant hiding at home with popcorn, waiting for the report.

The room was the same: folding chairs in a circle, fluorescent lights buzzing like hornets. Marlene smiled warmly. "Welcome back, Josh. And you brought family!"

"Unfortunately," I muttered as I took some lint off my blue jumper.

Claire shot me 'the don't start look.' Daniel just winked at me like he was about to audition for stand-up.

Maureen appeared instantly, perched in the empty chair beside me. She looked at Claire and Daniel, then back at me, grinning wickedly. "Oh, this is going to be fun. Tell them I'm here too. Let's see how they react."

I hissed, "Behave."

Marlene clapped gently. "Tonight, I'd like us to share not just about our grief, but about how our families are coping together."

Great. A family theme.

A silver-haired lady across the circle began, speaking tearfully about her late husband and how her daughter had moved back home to help her. Everyone nodded, dabbing their eyes.

Then Marlene's gaze landed on me. "Josh, would you and your children like to share?"

Claire sat straighter, pamphlet perfect. "Of course. We've been encouraging Dad to stay active, explore support networks, and keep a healthy routine."

Daniel muttered, "And stop yelling at appliances."

Maureen cackled. "Tell them you yelled at the toaster yesterday too!"

I almost said it aloud, but I caught myself just in time and faked a cough instead. Claire frowned at me.

"Dad?" Marlene prompted kindly.

I cleared my throat. "Yes. Well. My children, all three of them, mean well. They check on me. Frequently. Aggressively. But I'm fine. I talk things through."

"With whom?" Marlene asked.

There it was. The landmine.

"With..." I hesitated, eyes flicking to Maureen, who was now pantomiming blowing kisses to the kids. "...with myself. Internal dialogue. Very healthy."

Claire smiled politely, but her eyes screamed, 'We'll discuss this later'.

Daniel smirked. "He means Mum."

The group murmured sympathetically. Claire pinched the bridge of her nose.

"Tell them I still hog the bathroom," Maureen whispered gleefully.

And like an idiot, I repeated it—half under my breath. "She still hogs the bathroom."

Claire's head whipped toward me. "What?"

Daniel choked, trying to stifle laughter. "Dad, what—?"

I coughed again, violently. "Ha-ha, pollen season! Terrible this year."

Marlene, bless her, nodded sagely. "It's common to feel their presence in everyday routines. Even in bathrooms."

Claire looked like she wanted the floor to swallow her. Daniel was openly wheezing into his hands.

The session went downhill from there.

A man across the circle shared about how he still talked to his late wife's photograph every night.

Claire teared up. Daniel whispered, "Dad does that too, except he argues with her about vacuum lines."

I shot him a glare. Delighted, Maureen whispered, "Tell them he's right."

By the time Marlene wrapped up with a guided breathing exercise, Claire was stiff as a board, Daniel was snorting every 30 seconds, and I was sweating bullets trying not to blurt out anything ghost related. Meanwhile, said ghost was having the time of her afterlife.

As we filed out, Marlene stopped us at the door. "It was so wonderful to see you supporting your father. Grief is best carried together."

Claire nodded solemnly. "Yes. Together."

Daniel muttered, "Or in padded rooms."

Outside in the parking lot, Claire rounded on me.

"Dad. You cannot keep saying things like that in public. People will think—" She stopped, swallowing. "They'll think you're not okay."

Daniel added, "I mean, it is hilarious, but also? Kind of concerning."

I raised my hands. "I'm fine. Perfectly fine. I'm just remembering your mother. Aloud."

Claire sighed. "We'll talk about this later."

They drove off together, no doubt planning Intervention: The Sequel.

As soon as their car disappeared, I leaned against mine, exhaling hard. Then I laughed. A laugh that cracked into tears before I could stop it.

Maureen appeared at my elbow, glowing warmly. "Oh, Josh. You should've seen their faces. Absolutely priceless."

I wiped my eyes, still chuckling. "Congratulations. We're officially the most dysfunctional family in town."

She looped an arm around my shoulders or at least gave the ghostly impression of it. "Darling, we always were."

And I laughed again, tears blurring the parking lot lights, knowing she was right.

HOME VISIT

Just when I thought things couldn't get better I found out just how badly my kids had lost faith in me. How? By the reinforcements they'd sent directly to my lounge.

It happened on a Tuesday. I was in the middle of unloading the dishwasher (don't ask me about my ' technique' ; we've covered that battlefield) when the doorbell rang. Sophie stood there, wringing her hands, and beside her was… the group therapist. *My* group therapist. Clipboard in hand.

"Dad. I see you are wearing the blue jumper. As always," Sophie said nervously looking at Marlene, "I thought it might be nice if Marlene came by for a home visit."

"Nice?" I echoed. "Like a surprise colonoscopy is nice?"

Sophie gave me the 'don't embarrass me in front of company' look.

Marlene smiled serenely and stepped inside.

Now, you'd think this would be the perfect time for Maureen to behave. Keep quiet. Blend in. Let me pass as semi-sane.

But no.

She popped into existence the moment the door shut, perched on the arm of the sofa like a smug parrot.

"Oh, this is going to be rich," she whispered gleefully. "Tell her I haunt the laundry basket."

"Not now," I hissed.

"Sorry?" Marlene asked.

"Uh—cat hair. I get… a lot of cat hair."

I don't own a cat.

Marlene made a note.

Sophie led her in like a realtor showing off a property. "Here's the lounge. Dad spends most of his evenings here on the recliner. Watching TV. Reading."

Maureen leaned close. "Tell her you mostly argue with me about the remote."

I smothered a laugh and disguised it as a cough. "Yes. Very peaceful evenings."

We moved into the kitchen.

Marlene peeked into the open dishwasher. My proud, chaotic jumble of dishes sat like evidence at a crime scene.

"Josh," she said gently, "I notice the dishwasher is loaded creatively."

Maureen cackled. "Tell her it's modern art. Call it 'Ceramic Chaos No. 5.'"

Before I could stop myself, I blurted, "It's modern art!"

Both women turned.

I coughed. "Uh, well, my philosophy. Domestic expressionism."

Marlene nodded slowly, jotting something.

Sophie's face screamed, Oh God, he's doomed.

We moved to the laundry.

Bad idea.

The fitted sheet from my last solo attempt sat in a heap on top of the dryer, like a dead jellyfish.

"Ah," Marlene said delicately. "Struggling with sheets?"

Maureen leaned against the wall, laughing so hard she nearly phased through it. "Tell her it tried to strangle you!"

I chuckled nervously. "It puts up a fight sometimes."

Marlene nodded gravely, as though I'd just confessed to battling inner demons instead of elastic corners.

Finally, we ended up in the bedroom.

Big mistake, big mistake, a very big mistake.

Marlene's eyes fell on the two pillows: mine, flat and sad, and Maureen's, plump and untouched.

"You've kept her pillow," she said softly.

I froze.

Maureen slipped closer, her voice gentle now. "Tell her it still smells like me. Because it does."

My throat tightened.

For a second, I nearly said it. But then I saw Sophie watching me, her lip trembling, and I knew if I admitted that aloud, she'd break.

I cleared my throat. "Yes. I, uh, find it comforting."

Marlene smiled kindly. "That's healthy."

Maureen rolled her eyes. "Healthy? He drools on it sometimes. Puts it between his legs as if he is cradling my arse."

I snorted before I could stop myself.

Both women stared.

"Pollen season!" I blurted. "Terrible, isn't it?"

"You keep saying that, Dad, but I never known you to have allergies. What gives?" Sophie asked, demanded almost.

I just shrugged my shoulders.

Marlene made another note. Sophie rubbed her forehead.

The 'tour' wrapped up back in the lounge.

Marlene closed her notebook and gave me a look equal parts concerned and pleased. "Josh, I can see you're still very connected to your wife. That bond is beautiful, but you'll want to be mindful about distinguishing memory from presence."

"Presence?" I echoed.

"Yes," she said kindly. "Voices, sensations. Sometimes grief plays tricks."

Maureen leaned in, smirking. "Tell her I just pinched your bum."

I nearly yelped. Instead, I clapped my hands together. "Well! Coffee or a tea, anyone?"

Marlene declined, said she'd 'be in touch,' and finally left.

Sophie lingered by the front door, wringing her hands.

"Dad," she said softly, "please be honest with me. You're not actually hearing Mum, right?"

I looked at her—my sweet girl, her eyes full of worry—and forced a smile. "No, love. Just talking things through."

She nodded, hugged me tight, and left.

The moment the door shut, I collapsed into my recliner, laughter spilling out of me in helpless waves.

Laughter and tears are now always tangled together like they always are these days.

Maureen perched beside me, grinning. "Well, darling, congratulations. You've officially scared your therapist and our daughter."

I wiped my eyes, still laughing. "We're the craziest couple in town."

"Yes, we keep saying that to each other and we might just believe it." She kissed the air near my cheek, glowing softly. "And proud of it."

POPCORN NIGHT AND A GREY AREA

Friday was always a great day or night for me. Then, this Friday morning, in the space between brushing my teeth and deciding whether socks were worth the trouble, I realised I still had a key: Maureen and my old ritual.

Friday night, movies, and popcorn.

No matter how long the week had been, we would meet there. The world could wobble on its axis, but at 7PM, I would make sure the kernels went into the air-heated popcorn maker, and at 7:15PM, we would argue about subtitles.

I swept the bench counter, rinsed the plates, and placed them in the dishwasher (as newly instructed), then measured the oil like a chemist trying to impress a student. The kitchen ticked with the soft impatience of the wall clock.

Sunlight had by now disappeared and only the stand lamp gave a subtle light into the lounge. I opened the bag of corn kernels and dropped them into the small popcorn maker. The kernels fell clacking like castanets—and I felt something I hadn't in months: a hum. Not electricity. Anticipation.

"Going fancy?" Maureen said; hip against the counter, eyebrows arched and hair cascading down her shoulder, beautiful as always.

She moved from that position and perched on the stool in its soft glow, crossing one foot over the other. "Air-heated popcorn? Look at you, King of Chefs on a Friday."

"Pre-made microwave poppers are for cowards," I declared, nose high and proud. "And you always claimed the air-heated popcorn flew out of the little nozzle like a missile, that the air-heated little popper made it taste like a movie theatre, before they banned butter and joy."

She smiled the way she used to when I said something dumber than necessary.

"Here to supervise, are we?" I add.

"I'm here to steal the first handful," she said, and even the tease felt like a warm hand on my ribs.

I dropped a few test kernels in and waited for their little brave hearts to thump. The kitchen filled with the smell of corn futures, which brought a promise of warm salt and childhood. The air popper shook and made the sounds of a maraca with ambition as it filled the kitchen.

"Remember when you said the secret was faith?" I asked.

Maureen's chin lifted. "It always is. You put a lid on a rattling thing and trust heat to make it bloom."

The air popcorn maker went wild—pop, pop, pop, pop— a drum line in a metal helmet, and for a second, I swear I could hear her laughter braided through the sound. I tipped the white avalanche into our old stainless bowl, the one with the tiny dent.

"Salt?" I asked.

"And the good butter," she said. "Don't pretend to be healthy tonight."

I melted a knob until it went slick and gold, poured it through the sieve like an apology we'd both accept, and shook the bowl so the glitter got everywhere. I cracked a little black pepper on top because I felt like a chef narrating his own moves.

Maureen applauded with her eyes.

"What's the movie?" she asked as we moved toward the lounge.

The room had been tidied within an inch of its life, and I placed the remote where it couldn't humiliate me.

"I thought we'd expand your curiosity and education."

I held up the DVD I'd borrowed from the library, because at my age I still believed had things to learn: "Fifty Shades of Grey."

Her face went through a quick, delicious cycle: surprise, amusement, mock sternness.

"You're joking, and what are you hoping for when we watch this video?"

"I am very serious," I said, doing my best talk-show host voice. "A cultural phenomenon we skipped because we were busy having children and a mortgage."

"We saw the trailer once," she said, settling on our lounge, which still held what seemed like a million pillows as she motioned me to correct the pillows with a possessive ghost hand.

"I maintain that men in tight ties are suspicious," I replied, kissing the air an inch from her temple, because that was where my mouth knew to go.

She smiled more softly now. "Why this one?"

I didn't want to say, "because I miss wanting you and this might help," but that was what rattled under the lid. I cleared my throat. "Because it's Friday. Because popcorn. Because it's ridiculous. Because I am curious—don't tell me you weren't— and because I want to remember the electric parts."

Her eyes gentled. "Then press play, mister."

The studio logo rolled through icy skyscrapers and a soundtrack that tried too hard.

We leaned back.

I balanced the bowl between my ankles.

I could feel her not-weight along my side, how the couch subtly found the shape it had learned from us, even without her.

10 minutes in, I was heckling the architecture of the office building. 20 minutes in, Maureen was heckling the architecture of the contract. "Who negotiates clause 14 without snacks?" she muttered. "Bring a lawyer and a cheeseboard."

"Subtitles?" I asked. "I feel like we're missing nuance."

"The nuance is grey," she deadpanned. Then, softer, "You're stalling."

She was right.

Under the giggles and the bad dialogue, something had thrummed—an almost-forgotten engine catching after a long winter.

It wasn't the movie, not really.

It was the way she tilted her head over a line I knew she'd quote at breakfast.

It was the light behind the blinds.

The way my hand knew the route from her knee to her wrist.

The way our Friday nights used to draw a soft curtain around the house and tell the rest of the world to come back tomorrow.

On screen, two beautiful people pretended they were inventing desire. Beside me, desire had been invented long ago and was now returning from sabbatical with new stationery.

Maureen reached out, fingertips hovering just above my sleeve, like a bird that cared enough not to press its claws into bark.

"Do you remember," she murmured, "the time we paused Casablanca because you declared a national emergency in the kitchen?"

"Garlic bread," I said, smiling. "Sometimes you must."

"You came back smelling like a pizzeria," she said. "And somehow, that was romantic."

"It was the butter," I said gravely.

"It was you," she corrected.

The movie moved into its famous gear—whispers, silk, and music engineered to raise thermostats—and even though I wanted to laugh at the theatrics, part of me couldn't. Or rather, part of me didn't want to.

Because something had been waiting for permission. A door opened, and the room rearranged itself around breath.

I set the bowl on the table. The clink sounded too loud.

Maureen's eyes flicked to mine, and in that look, there was not a dare but an invitation as old as us, immediate as now.

"Josh," she said, and the way she said my name was the old way, how pulled grammar apart so it could touch the verb directly. "Go on."

"Are you sure?" I asked because I am, if nothing else, a gentleman who needed his ghost wife's consent.

She nodded, and the nod was both solemn and wicked, church and carnival. "I can't take part with you," she said, and the honesty stung sweetly. "But I'm here. I want you to feel alive. I want you to want."

"I do," I said, because the sentence had stored itself like conserved heat and I could finally release it. "I do."

I stood.

The room wobbled and then steadied, like the first moment of pushing off on a bicycle after 10 years of walking. I glanced back at her; she tilted her head toward the hallway—toward our bedroom.

We moved. Quietly, yes. Tense? Not exactly. More like tuning.

The bedroom had taken to staying tidy since she left; grief, for all its chaos, had made me neat. I switched the nightstand lamp on, and it seemed to light up like a low, late-summer setting.

The bed remembered our shapes.

The pillow she loved still wore the faintest shadow of her perfume—the kind that used to make mornings tilt toward mischief.

I sat on the edge, hands on my knees, feeling both 16 and a senator. She stood—no, hovered—in front of me, and I realised something I should have years ago: desire is less sight than sentence, less body than grammar.

It's the way a man and a woman turn into a 'we' and then split back to marvel at the seam.

"Tell me," I said. "Tell me what you'd say."

She smiled slowly, and it was the exact smile that had gotten us into good trouble a thousand times.

"I'd tell you to breathe," she said. "To take your time. To remember where I liked your hands. To remember that I liked you."

My chest lifted, fell. "Specificity helps," I murmured, and she laughed, low and fond.

"I'd tell you I love your shoulders when you think no one is looking," she said. "I'd tell you I love the way your mouth goes serious before it goes kind. I'd tell you to stop apologising with your eyes."

"I'd tell you," I said to her, suddenly brave, "that your hair always smelled like a conspiracy. That you could make a room blush by walking into it. That I never learned the map of you so much as learned the weather—where the rain fell, where the sun warmed, where the wind made sound."

"And I'd tell you," she said, voice dipping, "to be the man I know you to be."

The phrase hit me like a bell.

I put my hand on the mattress, palm flat, feeling the indent left by a life. "You make it easy."

"Now go on, Josh. Be alive." She said.

There was a way to describe what happened next that would involve the usual verbs.

I wouldn't use them. Not here.

Not that I was shy; it would be wrong to pretend the old language fit the new scenario.

What I could say was that I let the movie in the other room do its glossy business while I did mine: the business of remembering and inviting and not apologising to the air for wanting heat.

I closed my eyes and talked to her while I let my body be human.

I told her things I had been keeping like contraband: how the mornings hurt because the bed had been so cold during the night; how the evenings hurt because her recliner had too much echo; how I had feared desire because it felt like betrayal, and how I had now, finally, realised that desire in a kind of fidelity—fidelity to what we built, fidelity to the fact that my heart is not done wanting her.

She answered—in words, yes, and also in silences that felt like a fingertip pressed to my pulse.

She told me she loved me.

Over and over.

Not with fireworks but with a steady candle that refused to flicker out in a room.

She told me I was her man.

She told me not to be embarrassed by the noises a living body makes when it remembers it is not a museum.

She told me to meet her halfway across a bridge we couldn't see and wave with both arms.

I did.

There was a place in it that felt like cresting: the old bright edge where breath and prayer got easily confused. I thought of all our old jokes about synchronised watches and intermission snacks, and I laughed—a happy, breathless little laugh—and then I let the laugh melt into something softer.

Is it possible to have a private moment with a person you can' t touch?

Yes, I told myself.

Touch had always been more than skin.

It was sight, sound, and memories and the way your name felt in their mouth and the way your mouth learnt its way around their lips and eyes. It was the permission to be foolish and the bravery to be plain. It was the hands you wished you could hold guiding the hands you actually had.

When it was done—*if done is the word; I prefer arrived*—I laid back, dizzy and clear.

The lamp turned the ceiling into an old map.

In the bedroom doorway, I could see the narrow strip of light from the lounge, where our ridiculous movie continued without us, undeterred by our refusal to see it.

Maureen came closer, her glow gentled to a halo a choir might fight over. She sat—almost, always almost—beside me, and I felt the mattress give the faintest, impossible fraction.

"Hey," I said, smiling like a fool who'd passed an exam no one else had assigned him.

"Hey," she said back. There were 25 years of marriage in that syllable.

I turned my head to face her, which was a sentence that shouldn' t have been plausible and yet had always been the assignment.

"I'm sorry," I said.

"For what?" she asked softly.

"For wanting you," I said. "For thinking it was disloyal to want you like that."

Her eyes warmed. "Wanting or missing isn't disloyalty," she said. "It's grammar again. You're conjugating love in a tense you didn't expect to use."

"Present imperfect," I said.

She laughed. "Josh, my love, you were always imperfect. That was part of the attraction to you."

We lay there; not touching, as if I could touch her.

Innuendo owed its strength to the unsaid, and we had become very good at leaving room around words. Still, I said a few more: that she was beautiful, that I wanted her, again, that the wanting didn't bruise, that it buoyed.

"Good," she said. "Keep the wanting. Keep the Friday. Keep the popcorn."

"Even if I burn it?" I asked.

"Especially then," she said, with the sternness I married her for. "Burned edges are proof you turned the heat on."

We wandered back to the lounge because that was what people in love did: they returned to the scene of their rituals. The bowl waited, still half full, the pepper hiding like tiny freckles. I sat; she curled into the corner. On screen, two actors made a case for choreography. We made a case for choreography too, but ours involved a remote and a blanket and soft, stupid jokes.

"I think the writing could be better," I said.

"I think your acting was excellent," she replied, and I threw a kernel in her general direction. It passed through her and landed on the rug with a surrender that made us both giggle.

"Confetti," I said. "For surviving a winter."

"You're not done surviving," she said. "But you are done pretending you don't want spring."

I breathed.

That's all.

I breathed and noticed I was good at it again.

The room felt bigger, but not because I was small.

Because I could feel the corners again—the place where lamp met skirting board, where shadow met chair leg, where the wall remembered laughter like paint remembered hands.

"Thank you," I said.

"You're welcome," she said. "Always."

The credits rolled with the solemnity that movies gave themselves.

We stayed sitting until the screen went black and the room found its honest dark. When I switched the lamp off, the silence turned velvet instead of stone.

I walked her back down the little hallway because old habits gripped like ivy. At the bedroom door I paused and touched the frame the way I did when I wanted to make sure the house knew it was forgiven for hosting my sorrow.

"You know," I said, "you were right."

"About what?"

"About faith," I said. "You put a lid on a rattling thing and trust the heat to make it bloom."

She smiled, slow and pleased. "See? Popcorn as theology."

I leaned on the doorjamb; the old, dumb grin back because it had every right to be home. "The movie brought it out," I said. "The passion."

"It didn't bring it," she corrected. "It jiggled the lid."

I nodded. "Death didn't take it."

"No," she said. "It changed the room the passion lives in. But the room is still yours to enter."

"I miss you so much," I said, because the sentence was the spine; it held the rest of the body up.

"I know," she said, and that knowing wrapped around my ribs; made them less cage and more cradle. "I miss you too."

I stood there another minute, letting the air I'd warmed stay warm. Then I turned on the alarm system, and when I finally crawled into bed, I slid my hand across the sheet, palm open, like a man shaking hands with his own life. The cool cotton answered. Somewhere down the hall, the kitchen forgot to be lonely.

"Friday," I murmured to the ceiling.

"Friday," she agreed.

I slept like a person who had finally remembered something vital: that passion was not a visitor but a citizen, and grief couldn't revoke its passport.

I dreamed of kernels popping, one by one, and drifted into sleep with Maureen, as always, on my mind.

RED, YELLOW AND GREEN BINS

Monday afternoons in Northport, New South Wales, had a very particular soundtrack: magpies warbling like jazz critics, a mower coughing three houses over, and the squeak-squeak of plastic wheels as every driveway produces a bin in primary colours. Red for general. Yellow for recycling. Green for the sort of optimism I felt whenever I trimmed anything vaguely leafy.

I slipped on the Georgia Tech jumper—clean now, starch crisp as good manners—and rolled the red-lid out first. Maureen materialised beside me with the air of a supervisor caught mid-surprise inspection.

"Handle down so it doesn't run away," she said.

"It's a bin, not a greyhound," I muttered, but I flipped it anyway. Her approval landed like applause.

We did our little parade.

I popped open the yellow-lid and fished out an empty spaghetti jar I'd thrown in with the lid still on, already knowing what she was going to say.

"No lids," she tsked. "Rinse and separate. We're not animals."

"Yes, boss," I said. "Anything else while I'm re-sitting the Year Twelve recycling exam?"

"You've put a pizza box in there," she said, pointing with that sainted, spectral finger. "Grease, Joshua. That belongs in red."

"It's not grease, it's flavour residue."

"Red," she repeated, a judicial system in one word.

I swapped it across, and because I was in a good mood, I kept talking.

That's how it starts, isn't it? One minute you're chatting privately with your dearly beloved departed, the next you're hosting a one-man radio show for the street.

"You know," I said (aloud, apparently at medium theatre projection), "you're still bossy even in the afterlife."

Maureen grinned. "Project to the back row! The audience in the cheap seats can't hear you."

"Well, if they can't hear me by now—"

"Afternoon, Josh!" called Mrs Patel from the house to my right, pausing mid-hose. Water arced over her roses; a rainbow tried to form and then thought better of it.

I startled like a bin chicken caught in a bakery. "Afternoon! Lovely afternoon. Full of… dampness!"

I tried to make my face say "Bluetooth," patting my ear as though some invisible earpiece justified my public conversation.

My ear patted back: nothing. Of course.

From two doors down, Mr Pyle was trimming his verge with the intensity of a surgeon and the moustache of a man who'd won arguments with councils. He looked up, squinted, and started toward me, hedge clippers swinging like a villain's accessory. Behind him, his cattle dog, Bickie, grinned in the way all Australian dogs did when they were absolutely about to perform.

Maureen leaned in, delighted. "Oh, good. Witnesses."

"Don't you dare," I whispered.

"Who exactly are we not daring?" said Mr Pyle, now close enough to count the threads on my jumper.

His eyes did a quick scan of my face for wires. Finding none, his eyebrows did the heavy lifting. "You right, mate?"

"I am… spectacular," I said, and immediately wished I'd chosen a humbler adjective. "Just having a chat."

"On your own?" he said.

"With concepts," I said. "I'm rehearsing a podcast. Working title: Bins & Philosophers."

Mrs Patel had wandered closer, clutching her nose like a lie detector. "I thought perhaps you were on speaker?"

"Oh, no," I said. "This is vintage communication. Analog. I talk to the air; the air considers."

"Like prayer," she said kindly.

"Yes," I said, seizing the lifeline, "exactly like prayer, but with stronger views on pizza boxes."

"Lids off," Maureen chimed in, unable to resist.

"I heard that," I said aloud, unfortunately.

"You heard what?" said Mr Pyle.

"The magpies," I said. "Terrible this time of year. Very opinionated birds."

Bickie sneezed in a tone that suggested scepticism. A teenage boy on a bicycle flew past, looked at me, looked at the space next to me, and nearly rode into my yellow bin.

"Careful," I said to no one in particular.

"You sure you're alright?" said Pyle, softer now.

He and I had bonded once over a mutual hatred of televised cricket commentary, and he had that neighbour expression I recognise in the mirror: concern disguised as grumpiness.

"Saw you the other week shouting at your letterbox."

"That was a bee," I said. "We had differences."

He shifted, eyes catching on my jumper. "My Mavis had a cardigan she wore everywhere at the end," he offered, like a little flag of shared territory. "Said it made the days less echoey."

"It works," I said, equally soft. For a second, the footpath was a truce.

Then, the moment evaporated. I had to top it off with my mouth.

"Do you ever talk to her?" I asked before sanity could whack me with a rolled-up newspaper.

"Every day," he said simply. "But I don't do it on bin night in a voice like a town crier." He smiled to take the sting out. "Pop round for a cuppa if you like."

He and Bickie trundled back to their lawn.

Mrs Patel gave my arm a damp pat and returned to her roses.

The scooter kid executed a confused bunny hop and disappeared, no doubt to TikTok the saga of the Bin Prophet.

Maureen clapped without a sound. "10 out of 10. You're a neighbourhood feature now. Like the cockatoo that steals pegs."

"Wonderful," I said, gathering what remained of my dignity and wheeling the green-lid bin out to join its brothers. "I've become *that* man."

She cocked her head. "Which man?"

"The one who talks to the air," I said. "The eccentric widower. The local ghost whisperer."

"You say that like it's not the dream," she said. "Eccentric is just Latin for interesting."

"It's Latin for 'Claire will call within the hour'," I said.

We went back inside, and I tried to pretend I hadn't just given the street a free matinee. I made an espresso with my Lavazza pods. I stirred it as if stirring could fix anything. Maureen lounged against the fridge, delighted.

"Admit it," she said. "You enjoyed it."

"What—humiliation in public?" I stated.

"The show," she said. "That you were loud. The way they looked at you with curiosity instead of pity."

I opened my mouth to deny it, but she'd been my wife too long not to hear the truth first. The phone rang. I looked at her. She did the hand flourish that means, Go on, let's see the script.

"Hi, Dad," said Claire in that careful voice grown-ups use when removing glass from a cake. "Quick question."

"Before you ask, I did not yell at a letterbox today," I said.

A sigh. "Mr Pyle called."

"Ah. I bet he did."

"He said you were outside talking robustly," she said. "He thinks you might have 'gone peculiar.' That was his phrase."

I pinched the bridge of my nose. "Well, tell him congratulations on reading the minutes from last month's meeting."

"Dad."

"I'm fine," I said. "I just keep processing every day. Just processing. Talking things through with your mother."

Silence, then the sound of a daughter choosing one of seven responses and binning the other six. "Okay," she said finally, softening. "I love you. Just try to keep the volume to a dull roar in public?"

"I'll downgrade to a mutter," I said. "I'm auditioning for the Local Whisperer, anyway. Very prestigious role. I commune with bins."

She made a reluctant laugh, the kind that snags on worry.

"Daniel's coming over on Wednesday. Sophie's popping in tomorrow. No announcement, no agenda. Just popping. Please don't shout at the kettle."

"No promises," I said, and she laughed properly this time. We hung up.

I stood at the sink and watched a strip of cloud slide over the sun like a theatre curtain. Out on the kerb, the three bins glowed in their livery like well-behaved children waiting for the bus. Somewhere, a kookaburra found something hilarious about someone else's fence.

"You're a legend," Maureen said, one hand on her hip, her glow brighter for saying it. "The eccentric widower who talks to the air. The council will name a traffic island after you."

"Fantastic," I said. "I'll cut the ribbon with my sanity."

She floated closer, and for a second the kitchen felt like the old kitchen with new lighting. "You know what I like about today?" she said.

"My flawless PR with the neighbours?"

"That you didn't hide," she said. "You've tucked yourself into corners for months. Today, you stood in the middle of the street and were, well, you. Too loud, too honest, too alive."

I leaned on the bench, willing the kettle to finish its little drama. "And now everyone thinks I'm unspooling."

"Everyone already thinks something," she said. "Let them make it interesting."

I made us—me—coffee and carried it to the back patio because the afternoon did that late sun thing that makes even wheelie bins look cinematic. I sat. She sat near me or made the air sit. Across the fence, Mr Pyle's mower coughed into retirement, and I imagine his dog doing three ceremonial circles before collapsing into a contented sigh that could've been mine.

"Do you actually mind?" I asked finally. "About the reputation?"

"Of course not," she said. "You've always been my favourite weirdo."

"You Maureen, I'm not lonely. Not when you are here," I said, trying the sentence on like a jacket I'd forgotten I owned. "I'm an entertaining mystery."

"There you go," she said, proud of her student. "You're the subplot everyone gossips about at the letterbox."

"Until bin night next week when I debut my new material," I said. "A tight five on compost."

"You'll kill," she said. "Maybe literally if you talk about banana peels again."

We stayed there on the back patio while I enjoyed my coffee.

The next morning from my office window, I sat there soaking in the nothing-special of our neighbourhood that feels like everything. When the truck rumbled through after dawn with its huge 'hands' to pick up the bins and do its choreography of clunk and hiss, I waited until all three bins had been collected before I wheeled them back in. The street was getting ready for another day, and the scooter kid pointed me out to his friend and whispered, wide-eyed. Mrs Patel waved. Pyle gave me a nod that said, cuppa invitation still stands.

I am not who I was. I am not who they think I am. I am ⋯ becoming local folklore.

Inside, I dusted the jumper, smoothed it, and stood there a beat longer than necessary. "Next week," I said to the room, which was our room even when it was just mine. "I'll try the quiet version."

"Boring," Maureen sang. "But fine. We'll practice your whisper voice."

I grinned. "The bins will miss the show."

"They'll hear the encore," she said. "They always do."

I turned on the desktop computer, letting the house learn the hard drive starting up. I walked back into the lounge. The couch looked smug, like it knew our Friday had rearranged the future. In the hallway, the photos watched me like polite witnesses. At the bedroom door, I paused.

"You're not the lonely old man on the block," she said behind me, reading the thought I hadn't decided to have yet.

"No," I said, surprising myself with how easy the word came. "I'm an entertaining mystery."

"And legends," she said, "rarely whisper."

I dressed for my morning walk with her. Me in my cotton pants, Maureen in whatever a glow wore—with the soft rumour of the street slipping through the fly screen, I opened the front door. Somewhere, a bin lid clapped shut in the wind, like applause you didn't expect but take anyway.

THE NIGHT BEFORE

A few days went by in that strange, elastic way time had when you kept yourself busy on purpose. The bins did their weekly parade and returned like loyal dogs. The dishwasher and I negotiated another ceasefire. I even folded a fitted sheet that looked—if you squinted and believed—like a rectangle.

Then Monday turned to Tuesday, then Wednesday and so forth, and the house went quiet in a different register. The quiet that wasn't empty but expectant.

Tomorrow was our anniversary.

I didn't want company. I didn't want advice, not even from the glow of the woman whose advice I used to pretend to resent. I wanted something smaller. So, I did what we always did when the world felt too jagged: I went to the stereo.

It was the little silver unit we bought in that window of time when "compact" meant sophisticated and Bluetooth was a dentist. It clicked when you turned it on—a small, confident click, as if it was agreeing to keep your secrets. I pulled down the old CD wallet from the shelf—the one with her handwriting on Post-it notes—Our Wedding, underlined twice, and, in brackets, 'keep this safe, Josh'. (I didn't. She did. That was our whole marriage in three sentences.)

I slipped the disc in, and the tray slid shut with a whisper. In the lounge, the lamplight turned the walls the colour of honey. I left the blinds open so the light of the afternoon could sketch the neighbour's tree' s shadow through the lounge window. The air had that Northport coolness you only got after the heat had given up.

The first track found me standing without deciding to stand. I closed my eyes and swayed. It wasn't dancing, not the way we used to; it was the way a tree agreed with the wind. The opening bars were so familiar my chest knew them before my ears did. (We chose that song because she liked the singer; I liked the length—just enough to be romantic, not enough for me to overthink.)

I could smell the old perfume she wore on our wedding day because memory was the best contraband.

For a second, the lounge became that golf course again: late sun on stone, the fountain Tony insisted would be 'a brilliant spot for a photo.' (He was right, and I told him he'd never hear it from me. He heard it from me four million times after I saw it.)

We had stood by that fountain with our cheeks still pink after our commitment ceremony and saying, "I do." That photo was in the dining room now, big enough to be an extra guest at every meal.

I swayed, eyes closed, and she settled behind my eyelids exactly like she used to settle into my arms.

I didn't talk. Not at first.

This wasn't a summons.

The jumper—my ridiculous, beloved Georgia Tech jumper—hung on the back of the lounge chair like a loyal dog waiting for a walk, and my hands hovered over it once, twice.

I left it there.

I didn't put it on.

The moment was already holding me; I didn't trust myself to hold anything else.

The second song drifted in, and the room warmed.

I let my palms turn, as if they were resting on a waist that still knew my grip. I counted the rhythm the way she taught me—"Stop thinking, Joshua; your feet know the maths"—and I tried, I really tried, to let the maths do the job.

There was a prickle behind my eyes that I told myself was simply the lamp being sentimental. I breathed. In two, three; out, two, three. Somewhere beyond the glass, the magpies debated something vigorously and then decided the night deserved a vote of silence.

"Tony was right," I said finally at a volume no neighbour could complain about. "The fountain made us look like we knew what we were doing."

I could almost hear her grin. 'We knew,' she would have said. 'We just didn't know we knew.'

I didn't chase her voice. I didn't reach for the jumper. I stood there and let the music do the reaching. It wrapped the room in slow, soft fabric, and I swayed, and in the middle of the sway a thought presented itself, shy but insistent:

This was just a 'me' moment.

Not a 'we' moment.

Not a performance for the kids or the therapist or the street.

Not a proof of sanity.

Not a seance.

Just me, in our lounge, in the house we designed and built with our songs, on the night before the date that made the two of us official.

I kept whispering it as I moved, like a little spell: A 'me' moment. A 'me' moment.

It didn't feel like a betrayal.

It felt like the kind of permission she would have written on a shopping list between milk and coriander.

The third song was the one we used to butcher at home, turning it into a slow-motion shuffle. I let myself smile, because my body remembered the dumb dip I always attempted and how she'd yelp and laugh and then pretend to dock my points like a judge on television. I let myself miss the way her hair would tickle my lip. I let myself miss it without apologising to the ceiling for wanting it back.

Halfway through, the stereo did that tiny whirr it did when it decided the laser needed a breather. I stopped moving.

The house breathed with me.

I looked toward the dining room doorway where the photo hung—that frozen laughter by the fountain. For a mad split second, I wanted to take it down and hold it like an album cover while I finished the dance, but even I knew I wasn't strong enough for that kind of theatre.

Instead, I turned slowly so I could face it as I swayed. We looked at each other—me and the picture—and that was enough. The next track stole in, and I let my eyes close again.

Everything slowed when you shut your eyes: the air, the uncertainty, the ache. You could put your ear against the day and hear the hours inside it.

"I miss you heaps, baby," I said, because the room already knew.

Saying it aloud made the floor steadier under my socks.

"Tomorrow's ours."

No voice answered.

No glow.

Just the music.

And the music was kind. It said: *Yes. And yes. And keep moving, old boy; you ' re doing fine.*

A shiver went through me from the base of my neck to the soles of my feet; the kind that wasn't cold.

I thought of the jumper again and knew if I put it on, I would fall apart exactly the way the good plates fell apart that one Christmas. I thought of calling Claire, or Sophie or even Daniel, of announcing something I couldn't possibly translate.

I thought of the fountain and Tony's grin and the way the photographer told us to "just be yourselves" and how Maureen whispered, "Lucky for him, we don't know how to be anyone else."

Maybe I said some of that aloud.

Maybe I didn't.

The stereo clicked over to the last song, the one we chose because it sounded like sunrise. I moved less now, more a sway than a dance, and I let the last minutes do what last minutes do: gather and bless.

When it finished, the little unit gave its polite sigh, and the room expanded to normal size again. I took out the CD, and I stood in the middle of the lounge and listened to the fridge hum. The silence after music always had a shape.

Tonight, it was a circle.

I stepped out of it and went to the dining room. I stood in front of the fountain photo and let my eyes go soft enough to pretend it was a window.

"Tomorrow," I said to them—those two people with silly grins who did not know what they were promising and promised it, anyway.

"I'll buy you flowers even though you never liked me to because you always felt they would be a waste. You prefer them to be left in the fields living, not plucked and placed in a vase. I'll make the coffee too strong and pretend that's on purpose. I'll take the long way on my walk and say hello to the pond where the ducks are and tell them, if they' re there, that you say hello too."

I rested my fingertips on the frame, just the way you might pat a shoulder on your way passed, and returned to the lounge. I passed the recliner with the jumper waiting on it and let my hand hover in the air above it, a benediction without contact. Then I curled up on the sofa, still warm from the dancing, and pulled the throw over my knees.

For a minute, I imagined what tomorrow would bring.

Maybe one of the kids would remember the date at breakfast; maybe not.

Maybe the therapist would call to "check in"; maybe I'd let it go to voicemail and reply with a thumbs-up that said nothing and everything.

Maybe I'd take a sticky note and write Fountain in capital letters and stick it on the front door like a compass.

Maybe I'd do nothing, and that would be fine because grief was not a schedule; it was like the weather.

I let the house go darker as the sun set and sat there as the room got darker. The stereo's little orange LED was the last thing awake in the room. I could imagine the trees outside in the park swaying in the wind, and I rested. When I finally got up and turned that light off too, the lounge returned to being what it was at midnight: a memory you could sit in.

At the bedroom door I paused, looked again at the jumper, and shook my head.

Not tonight.

Tonight, had been a 'me' moment.

She would have smiled at that if I had told her. She would have teased me for saying it aloud like a headline. And then she would have told me to brush my teeth and stop being philosophical with popcorn breath.

"Bossy," I whispered, smiling despite myself.

I climbed into bed and let the cool sheet find my knees, my shins, the curve of a day that had finally learned to be quiet.

In the morning, I would wake and make coffee, decide about flowers, and walk past the dining room. I would nod at the fountain and the two people laughing in front of it.

Tonight, I let the music that was no longer playing keep playing, anyway.

Tomorrow is the day.

Our day.

I let my eyes close around that fact until it was gentle enough to sleep with.

And just before I slipped under, the thought returned, clearer for being simple: *This is just a me moment.*

It didn't make the missing smaller.

It made the missing mine.

And tomorrow, when I stood by whatever fountain I could find—stone or memory—I'd bring that with me like a vow you repeat to yourself because it still fit.

I heard the house breathed. I breathed with it.

Somewhere far off, a car door shut, and a dog decided the night was acceptable. I heard it because I'd left the bedroom window slightly open like Maureen used to. I smiled into the dark and dreamed of the sound a dress made when it raced a fountain to the punchline, and of the way a song, once yours, never left.

"Good night, my love," I whispered. "Tomorrow, I will

ANNIVERSARY WITH EXTRAS

I woke up already dressed for the day. Some mornings took negotiation; this one stood there at the foot of the bed and said, 'Well?'

Anniversary.

I made the coffee that could apologise on my behalf and drank it at the dining table beneath the big photo: two foolish people by a fountain, not yet skilled at anything except promising.

Tony had been right about the fountain ("Mate, it's a brilliant spot"), and I had told him he would never hear those words from me. He'd heard them six times before dessert.

By mid-morning I'd decided on flowers.

Supermarket bouquets have always been my spiritual home, but I drove to the proper florist at the Narellan shopping centre, the one with the chalkboard out front that said things like 'Peonies are back! Like it's a sequel'. I stood in front of the glass vases, auditioning their contents. She never liked lilies—"funeral flowers," she'd said, and then patted my cheek for thinking them elegant—so I chose a straightforward choice of white carnations and one long-stemmed rose in the middle because even I believe in clichés on our day.

"Occasion?" the florist asked, tying the ribbon.

"Anniversary," I said.

"Congratulations," she said, and I didn't correct her.

I came home with my bouquet and my ridiculous grin and set to work on the theatre of evening. I ironed a tablecloth badly enough to remind the cloth who was in charge. I brought out the good plates and the good cutlery and the cheaper wine glasses that didn't give me a panic attack when I breathed near them. I lit three candles—one short, one tall, one ridiculous—and put them in a row like a chorus line.

The Georgia Tech jumper hung over the chair back like a decision. I tried not to make a ceremony of it, then failed, and put it on. The weight settled in the surrounding air, as it always did. I waited for a moment, but when she didn't appear I knew why. She was letting me do this on my own; giving the moment, the day, the air it deserved.

I set the flowers in the old jug we used to call "the posh one" because it didn't have cartoon ducks on it. The house smelled of carnations and memories.

By six, the day had started its long, honey-coloured slide into dusk. Magpies called their evening notes up the street; with the patio door open, I could hear a car door slam shut.

I stood in the lounge doorway and did the inspection a man did when he was pretending to be casual but was actually bracing every muscle. Candles steady. Music quiet. Table set. Photo watching.

Then the lights flickered. Not a brownout—just a quick wink, as if the house had a joke to share and wasn't sure I could take it. The candles fluttered and steadied; the shortest one guttered out.

I looked up.

She was there—soft glow, faint smile, mischief at the edges.

"No open flames without supervision," Maureen said, in that stern tone she used whenever I got romantic with matches.

"You and the fire brigade," I said. "Always cramping my mood lighting."

She glanced at the candles again and one trembled, then settled lower, the wick a tiny coal. "Call it assisted exhale," she said.

"Show-off."

She perched on the armrest of the dining room chair like a queen in exile and let me look at her. There was a hush to these arrivals I still hadn't learned not to fill with chatter, so I didn't talk. I stood there and let the jumper be what it was: a seat belt and a scandal sheet. The house breathed again. Outside, the gum swayed, and dusk gathered speed.

"Happy anniversary!" she said softly.

"Happy anniversary! Yes, right back at ya!" I smiled.

We did what we've always done when the date was bigger than the room: we told stories until it fit.

I poured us—me—some sacramental wine from Costco that she loved, and she watched with that look she saved for my attempts at class. We sat, me in the chair, her a careful brightness beside it, and I started with the part that has become a legend in our family.

"Your mother," I said, and that was enough to make her laugh aloud.

"Poor Mum," she said, not sorry at all.

"Poor pokie machine," I corrected, "when she marched into the casino because she was not happy about you leaving for America with me and needed an argument with a machine instead."

"She didn't march," Maureen protested, delighted. "She pouted at speed."

"She vanished like a magician," I said. "One minute she's at the table, poking at the prawns. The next minute she's gone and Tony's looking under the tablecloth like she's hiding there."

"She came back with a coin cup," Maureen said, "and said, 'If you're going to run off to America with this one, at least I'll have entertainment while you're gone.'"

"And I said, 'I can juggle,' and she said, 'That's not what I meant.'"

We laughed in the way married people laugh when protecting a third party they adore—a mixture of fondness and mockery and gratitude for having all three.

"And you," she said, pointing a ghost finger that still knew how to accuse, "danced like a giraffe learning to ice skate."

"I was nervous," I protested. "My hands were sweating so much the ring nearly floated off in its own boat."

"You counted out loud," she said, eyes sparkling. "One-two-three, sorry, one-two-three, sorry again."

"I don't deny the apology," I said. "I believe they mislabelled the rhythm."

"You stepped on my toes," she said.

"I *cherished* your toes," I said, which is what husbands say when cross-examined.

She leaned back, smiling faintly—a smile that lived somewhere between a smirk and a benediction.

"You made me laugh," she said. "You always make me laugh. That' s what I love about you. And you let me be me. I had never felt more confident, more secure than when I was with you, Josh."

"Non-refundable forgiveness," I said.

"Lifetime warranty," she said.

We ate the easiest dinner I could manage without a second adult in the kitchen—bread that pretended to be artisan, tomatoes that had seen salt, and cheese that made you negotiate. We toasted the fountain, the photo, the poor prawns at the commitment ceremony dinner, and Tony' s eternal correctness. We toasted her mother, who did not smile in the photos but pressed a ten-dollar note into my hand as we left for the hotel and said, "For snacks, if she makes you hungry." We toasted the years we built from nothing but optimism and stubbornness and the occasional laminated instruction booklet.

At some point I realised I was both aching and lit from the ribs out. Grief and gratitude, the house specialty. I stood, set my glass down, and the words rose as if they had been practicing in my throat all afternoon.

"Happy anniversary, my love," I whispered.

Silence said it back.

Not because there was no reply, but because some replies are heavier than words.

The jumper held me steady.

The candles nodded like old friends approving of our choices.

The room went almost silent.

I crossed to the stereo, the silver one with the polite click and the orange eye, and pressed play. The music started, and it was more alive than last night—as if the machine had given the songs their youth back for the evening. I stood in the middle of the lounge, let the first bars find me, and then I did the only sensible thing: I danced.

"Careful," Maureen warned, delighted. "The table's close."

"You're close," I said, already laughing through a throat that didn't know whether to open or close.

We swayed—me with gravity, her with whatever physics had to say about devotion—and by the second chorus I was grinning and sniffling in the same breath. The track changed. I tried a little flourish I had no business attempting. She made the face she used to make when I reached for the dip.

"You're still stepping on my toes," she said, "even without touching me!"

I barked a laugh, then choked on it, then laughed again because this was what we did: we took the ridiculous by the hand and gave it a place at the table.

Tears kept coming anyway. I let them. They made a pleasant rhythm, pattering small and warm. I could have sworn she rolled her eyes at my timing, and I loved her for it.

When the song tapered, I didn't stop. I kept moving, small circles in a room that knew the map of our feet. I leaned my cheek toward where her hair should have been and said, softer than the stereo, "Thank you for still being here."

She didn't make a joke.

She didn't make me deflect. She just answered, voice low and clear enough to settle an argument with the sky. "I will be here until I am no longer needed."

I froze. Not from fear — astonishment had its own stillness.

The candles hummed.

The jumper tightened like a hand. I didn't ask the next question, the one about who decided and when; I held the sentence she'd given me like a glass of water in a drought. Then, I did the only thing that made sense in a room with flowers and music and a history of foolishness.

"Will you marry me again?" I asked.

She smiled. It started at the corner and moved inward — the same route it took the first time I saw it. "Yes," she said, as if there had been no other answer. "Yes."

The stereo nudged the next track into being, and the house, ever obedient, became a chapel made of carpet and shadows from the three uneven candles. I swayed, and she swayed in the way she could, and the fountain in the photo seemed to catch the light differently, as if it had made a small, private rainbow at our table.

We didn't speak after that for a while.

We let the songs be the vows and the silence be the amen.

When the disc clicked to a stop, I stood there with my eyes closed long enough to feel the after-music settle into my ribs. Then I blew out the two remaining candles with more ceremony than I intended and watched the smoke write brief cursive on the dark.

I carried the flowers to the bedroom because I could; I set one carnation in a glass by her pillow; I folded the tablecloth into its usual wonky square because imperfection was how we knew whose house this was. I came back to the lounge and took off the jumper. I set it over the chair like I was saying goodnight. The air cooled my cheeks, and it felt like permission to sleep.

I looked at the photo again in the dining room.

There we were, two people by a fountain, laughing at something I could no longer quite hear, swearing to things we imagined and then made. I saluted them with two fingers, like a soldier who'd finally learned his post.

"Happy anniversary," I said again, and let the house answer the way houses did; with a hush and a held breath.

In bed, I lay on my side and looked at the space where she would be, and, for once, the space did not look like a hole. Tonight it felt like a harbour.

Somewhere outside, the neighbour's dog told another car off, and the car apologised by driving away. I laughed once, quietly, at nothing and everything.

Then I whispered into the dark—because this was what we had always done on this date, even if we forgot to say it out loud—"I choose you," and I thought I heard, "I choose you" returning from a place without walls.

It was tender, and it was ridiculous.

It was devastating and unforgiving in the same minute.

It was corny tonight, but I told myself: tonight, it was ours.

And I slept that night with gratitude warming the small of my back, the jumper always within reach in case I wanted to see her again, the music still playing in my mind where no one could hear it, the yes echoing like a bell rung only once and then listened to for years.

"Happy anniversary, my love. Thank you for all the wonderful years. I miss you so much, but I thank you for being here tonight."

As I closed my eyes, I had only one thought in my mind.

What did Maureen mean by her statement?

"I will be here until I am no longer needed."

A SANDWICH AND A COFFEE

I walked into the Northport Café that afternoon, not because the house was suffocating me, but because I was—dare I say it—curious about being among people again.

The group therapy had been good.

Strange, but good.

I wasn't spilling my guts every session, but I was listening, learning, and, for the first time in months, I wasn't afraid of my own thoughts. The kids noticed. Claire even joked that I'd officially graduated from the "fast track to the looney bin."

That one stung, but it came with a smile and a hug, so I let it pass.

I was wearing the old blue Georgia Tech jumper. Faded, frayed at the cuffs, probably one wash away from disintegrating—but it was mine, and it was my armour. I pushed open the café door, bells jangling like a comedy sound effect.

Helen, the owner/barista, looked up from behind the espresso machine. She was in her mid-40s, maybe, with hair tied back in a messy bun and the kind of energy that made a person feel instantly welcome.

"Well, hello there," she said. "I haven' t seen you before. What can I get you? Besides a refill of that smile—you've got a good one."

I actually blinked.

Did she just…? Yes. Compliment delivered. With froth, no less.

I managed a half-smile back. "Uh, coffee. Flat white. And maybe a sandwich, whatever's least likely to kill me."

She laughed. "Ham and cheese it is then, with a bit of salad on the side. Don't worry, I test everything on myself first. You'll survive."

I sat at a corner table.

When she brought my order over, she lingered, leaning against the counter like we were already mid-conversation.

"So," she said, eyes twinkling, "what's with the jumper? Looks like it's been loved half to death."

I opened my mouth to take a sip of the coffee when—

"Oh, please," Maureen muttered in my ear. "She's flirting like a seagull after chips."

I nearly inhaled the coffee.

Coughed so hard my eyes watered.

Helen immediately rushed to my side, thumping my back. "Whoa, easy there! Are you okay? Didn't think my flat white was that strong!"

I croaked out, "Fine, fine—wrong pipe."

Meanwhile, I could practically feel Maureen crossing her ghostly arms and tapping her invisible foot.

Helen smiled sympathetically. "Happens to the best of us. I'll grab you some water."

As soon as she turned, I hissed under my breath, "Maureen! What was that for?"

"What was what for?" she shot back. "I have every right to haunt the dating scene. And she was practically batting her eyelashes into your cappuccino foam."

"I am not *dating*," I muttered. "I'm just having a sandwich and a coffee. Are you now jealous?"

"No," Maureen remarked, but her eyes said something else.

Helen returned with water, mistaking my muttering for nerves.

"Don't worry," she said kindly, "I don't bite. Unless you want me to." Then she winked.

I almost sprayed water across the table.

Maureen groaned like a stage actress in a tragic play. "Oh, perfect," she said. "You've got the flirtatious widow-whisperer on one side, and me on the other, reminding you I'm still here. Enjoy your sandwich, Casanova."

I rubbed my forehead. "I'm not Casanova," I mumbled.

Helen laughed again, clearly thinking I was making a joke at my expense. "Modest too. I like that."

I didn't know whether to laugh or bolt for the door.

My dead wife was sulking in one ear, while a very alive barista circled like a hawk in the other.

And for the first time, it hit me.

Maybe Maureen wasn't ready to let go.

Maybe I wasn't either.

But what did that mean for me—for us?

I chewed on the ham and cheese, stared at the steam curling up from my cup, and thought, *I'm not ready to date. But I'm also not ready to be haunted into celibacy.*

"Don't you dare," Maureen muttered.

"Don't I dare what?" I whispered.

"Smile back at her like that. You're mine, jumper and all."

Helen tilted her head, misinterpreting the words as directed at her. "Well, thank you," she said with a playful grin.

I groaned.

My life had officially become a sitcom—except the laugh track was in my head.

The moment I could I left the café and headed home. Maureen was nowhere to be seen—she'd left the moment I'd walked out the café door—so as soon as I arrived, I took the time to myself and ran with it. I took off my jumper and sat in my reading recliner to think of what had happened just now.

Maureen, well, seemed jealous, or not ready for me to move on, or what I was not sure. I decided not to think any more about what had happened and just get some emails done.

Later that evening, the house was calm. I had a group phone call, and each kid was in their own place when I called to connect with them. Sophie, with her earbuds listening to music, answered singing; Daniel was glued to the PlayStation but still picked up, while Claire was drafting another lecture to make sure I didn't go off the rails again.

Well, that was what I thought when she answered and said, "Hold on, Dad, I just need one more minute to write an idea."

The call went well.

"Just reporting in," I said, and they were happy to hear me say I was well, and after a few minutes they each hung up and went their merry way.

I went into the bedroom with the lamp on low, the old blue jumper still clinging to the back of the chair where I had placed it earlier. I could smell faint traces of coffee on the sleeve—Helen's café had somehow followed me home.

I took the jumper, put it on and leaned back against the headboard. "All right, Maureen. Spill it."

She appeared as she always did when I called—not with a bang or a puff of smoke, but simply there. Quiet, arms folded, eyebrows raised like she'd been waiting for me to admit what was already obvious.

"You don't want me to move on, do you?" I asked. My voice was steady, but my chest felt like someone had stuffed it with lead.

Her lips pressed into a thin line. Then: "Move on? Already? You choke on one coffee and let a woman wink at you, and suddenly it's dating season?"

I sighed. "I didn't say I was moving on. I said you don't want me to. That's different."

She sat down on the edge of the bed, though the mattress didn't dip. It never did. She stared at her hands, then back at me. "You're right. I don't want you to."

I swallowed. "Why?"

Her answer wasn't quick.

Usually, Maureen was fast with a quip, a jab, or a sarcastic remark. Tonight, she paused—like she had to dig for words she didn't want to give.

"Because if you move on," she said finally, voice soft, "I disappear. Not just this—" she waved at herself, shimmering faintly like a reflection in water—"but *me*. Us, everything we had. It'll get overwritten."

"Overwritten?" I almost laughed, but it came out too sharp. "You think loving someone new erases you? As if all our years of marriage just get deleted like a terrible draft?"

Her eyes glistened. "Doesn't it?"

The silence stretched.

I thought of Helen's easy laugh, of the way she'd leaned in with a spark of possibility.

And then I thought of Maureen, her terrible jokes, her morning grumbles, her uncanny way of knowing exactly how much milk I liked in my tea without asking.

I leaned forward, elbows on my knees. "You're here," I whispered. "Even when I try not to think about you, you're *stitched into me*. I can't delete you from me anymore than I could a vital organ. Moving on doesn't mean moving away. It just means I'm still alive."

She looked at me for a long time.

Then she smiled—faint, bittersweet, the way she used to after we argued and made up.

"Well," she said, "don't expect me to clap when the barista writes her number on your takeaway cup, but I would like you to ask for permission to move on when you are ready."

I chuckled, the sound catching in my throat. "Deal."

We sat together in the half-light—me on the bed, her on the edge of memory—and I realised for the first time that maybe letting go wasn't the same as being forgotten.

IDEA FROM THE THERAPY GROUP

The following Wednesday, I shuffled into the circle at therapy like a schoolkid dragging himself to detention.

Plastic chairs, lukewarm coffee in the corner, that familiar smell of disinfectant and hope.

"Good to see you, Josh," said Martin, our group leader. He was one of those unnervingly calm men who looked like he'd meditated through a car crash. "How's your week been?"

I hesitated.

The old me would have said, Fine. No complaints. Move along, please. But group therapy had a way of squeezing the truth out of you, like toothpaste you didn't know you had left.

I cleared my throat. "I, uh… nearly died."

The group leaned forward in perfect unison. You'd think I'd announced a winning lottery ticket.

"Coffee incident," I explained quickly. "Choked. Northport Café. Owner thought I was nervous. My wife thought the owner was flirting."

A beat of silence.

Then laughter bubbled around the circle.

"Wait," said Karen, the one with the sharp bob haircut, always the first to call out nonsense. "Your wife?"

I winced. "Ex-wife. No, sorry. Late wife. Deceased wife." I waved my hand. "She's haunting me. Don't worry, it's casual. Strictly no head-spinning or pea soup."

More chuckles. Except Martin, who nodded like I'd just confessed to a minor addiction. "Tell us about the café, Josh."

I sighed. "Look, I was just having a sandwich. Ham and cheese and a coffee. Safe choice, right? Then the barista, Helen, smiles, she jokes, she flirts. Which I didn't ask for, mind you. And suddenly Maureen's whispering in my ear like a jealous teenager. Next thing I know, I'm coughing up a lung, Helen thinks she's killed me, and I'm sitting there arguing with thin air about fidelity and ham and cheese sandwiches."

The group roared. Even Martin cracked a smile.

"And how did that make you feel?" he asked, voice calm again.

"How did it make me feel?" I rubbed my temples. "Like I'm dating with a referee. Like I can't even look at a waitress without Maureen rolling her eyes from the great beyond. And here's the kicker: I realised maybe she doesn't want me to move on. Maybe she's scared she'll vanish if I do."

The laughter softened. Heads tilted. The air got heavy.

"That," said quiet little Dave, the widower of three years, never spoke over two sentences, "sounds bloody exhausting."

I barked out a laugh, then surprised myself by tearing up. "Yeah. It is."

Martin leaned in. "Josh, you're carrying guilt for being alive. That's not unusual. The question is, do you want to keep living like that, or do you want to give yourself permission to live *with* Maureen's memory instead of *for* it?"

The words hit me like a slap.

Permission. I'd never thought about it that way, and Maureen even said I should ask her before moving on.

The group sat in silence, waiting for me.

And for once, I didn't deflect with a joke. I just nodded. "Maybe it's time I asked her for it."

The group nodded in agreement, and just then Marlene walked in.

"Okay people. Let us get started. Who wants to go first?"

I smiled to myself; the group—or maybe just me—had made more progress in those few moments before she walked in that Marlene had in multiple sessions.

Nothing like having people who'd gone through the same issues as you to help you through it.

CLAIRE'S ANGER

Claire turned up on Saturday afternoon, unannounced. She's always been the practical one—the schedule keeper, the worrier, the one who sends texts like "Remember, Dad, it's bin night" as though I'd suddenly forgotten how to live in a house.

Before she arrived, I was in the lounge, talking low. Maureen was perched in her usual corner of the sofa. We were having one of our circular conversations—I'd been pushing again, asking her if she'd ever really want me to be happy with someone else, and she was dodging, deflecting.

"Joshua," she said—still calling me that instead of Josh, like she always had when she wanted to make a point. "Just— just listen for once—"

"Dad?"

Claire's voice cut across mine.

I turned, startled, and there she was, standing, hearing me argue with her mother, with her bag slung over her shoulder, face pinched with that look of exhausted disappointment she used to save for Daniel's failed homework.

"What are you doing?" she asked.

I froze. My hand was half-raised, palm out, as though I was trying to calm Maureen. To Claire, I must've looked like a lunatic, scolding empty space.

"I was just—"

"Talking to Mum." The words spat out of her mouth like a bullet. "You were talking to Mum."

I opened my mouth to explain, but nothing came. What could I say? 'Yes, darling, your dead mother drops by for coffee and to critique my beard.'

She dropped her bag with a thud.

"I thought you were better than this. Moving on, Dad. That's what you keep telling us about the therapy sessions, isn't it? That you're, okay? But you're not! You're here pretending she's not gone, and it's—" Her voice cracked. "She's gone, Dad! She's *gone!*"

The room vibrated with her grief, sharper than my own. I reached for her, but she stepped back, shaking her head.

"Stop pretending," she said, low now, her face blotchy with unshed tears. "Please."

Then she turned, grabbed her bag, and was out the door before I could find the words.

The silence left in her wake was unbearable. I turned slowly. Maureen sat there, her hands clasped tight in her lap, for once without a single quip perched on her tongue.

"She doesn't understand," I whispered.

Maureen's voice was soft, almost breaking. "She shouldn't have to."

I blinked at her.

Her eyes lifted to mine, shimmering. "Watching her like that—watching them like that—it hurts more than I thought it would. I can't... I can't even hold her. Can't tell her it's okay. She's *grieving me*, Josh, and I'm still here—but not in any way that helps."

It hit me hard, a weight in my chest I hadn't prepared for. I'd been so tangled in my struggle–Holding on, letting go, hearing her voice, seeing her face–that I'd forgotten our kids were stuck in the middle of it. Pulled between the memory of their mother and the presence of their father who looked like he'd lost his grip.

For the first time since she came back to me, Maureen looked smaller, fragile in a way I'd never seen her.

She whispered, "I thought this was just about you and me. But it's not, is it? It's about them too."

I pressed my hands to my face.

The truth was unbearable. Claire's words still rang in my ears: *She's gone, Dad. Stop pretending.*

But Maureen wasn't gone—not to me.

Not yet. And maybe that was the problem.

BECOMING A SINGLE PARENT

I didn't sleep that night. The house felt raw, like the walls themselves had soaked up Claire's words and were echoing them back at me.

She is gone, Dad. Stop pretending.

By morning I knew I couldn't leave it hanging.

Claire was the one who'd always been closest to her mum—same stubborn streak, same way of tucking her hair behind her ear when she was annoyed. If I lost her now, if she thought I was cracking up beyond repair, I didn't know how we'd patch things back together.

I drove to her unit in Elderslie, the town over.

I stopped twice on the way because my hands wouldn't stop trembling on the steering wheel.

She answered the door in sweats, eyes swollen.

She didn't invite me in, but she didn't slam the door either, so I took that as progress.

"Can we talk?" I asked.

She crossed her arms. "About what? About how you and Mum had coffee yesterday and you still wear that damn blue jumper today?"

Her sarcasm stung, but I deserved it.

I nodded toward the hallway.

"Please, Claire. Just give me 10 minutes. If you still think I'm crazy afterward, I'll shut up forever."

She sighed and then stepped aside.

Inside, her place smelled like candle wax and laundry powder. I sat gingerly on the edge of her sofa. She perched opposite, arms still folded, waiting like a prosecutor.

I took a breath.

"You're right. She's gone. I know that. I went to the funeral. I saw the coffin. I've been living in this house without her for months, and every corner feels wrong. So, believe me—I know she's gone."

Claire's expression softened just a fraction.

"But sometimes," I went on, "it's like she's still with me. Not in a spooky, rattling-chains way. More like… my head stitching her into the quiet. I hear her voice, Claire. I see her sitting there. And I talk back because—" I broke off, rubbed my hands together. "Because I don't know how not to."

Her eyes flicked down, then up again. "Dad, that sounds like you're holding on too tight."

"Maybe I am." My throat thickened. "But it doesn't mean I'm pretending she didn't die. It means I'm still learning how to live with it. And I'm not asking you to play along. I just—" My voice cracked. "I just don't want you thinking I've abandoned reality. Or abandoned you."

For the first time since yesterday, her shoulders slumped.

She leaned forward, elbows on her knees. "You scared me. That's all. Seeing you talk to thin air like that, I thought, what if I've already lost him too?"

The words gutted me.

I reached across the coffee table, not sure if she'd let me, but she did. Her hand slipped into mine, warm and shaking.

"You haven't lost me," I said. "I'm still here, baby. Messy, maybe, but here. And I'll keep working on it. The therapy—all of it. For you, for your brother and sister. For Mum too, in a way."

Her eyes filled.

She nodded, silent tears rolling.

And for the first time in months, I felt like we were both grieving together instead of on opposite sides of a wall.

When I left her place later, I caught a flicker of Maureen in the rear-view mirror. She wasn't smirking or teasing. Just watching, quiet, her eyes glistening like Claire's had.

"Thank you," she whispered.

And for once, I didn't know if she meant for me, or for our daughter.

After the talk with Claire, things felt lighter between us—not fixed, not perfect, but lighter. I drove home with the strange relief of a man who'd been holding his breath too long.

But if there was one thing grief had taught me, it was that it didn't stick to one person at a time.

It seeped. It spread.

And my other two kids were carrying it in their own ways.

Daniel was first. I went to visit him at his place. I knocked, and I saw he had his headset on. I could imagine him muttering at the screen in that sharp, competitive voice he used for his games. "Move, idiot! No, left—oh, for God's sake, revive me, revive meeeeee."

Once he saw me, he ripped the headset off and groaned.

"Rough match?" I asked, sinking into the recliner.

He shrugged, avoiding my eyes. "It's just… whatever. It doesn't matter."

I wanted to tell him it did matter, that his sudden obsession with the PlayStation was more than just a hobby — it was his way of filling silence. But I didn't. Instead, I walked to his lounge and sat down, and I leaned forward. "You know, I used to get this mad at Pac-Man. Your mum would laugh until she cried watching me throw the controller."

That got a tiny smile, the first flicker of warmth I'd seen in weeks. He looked at me like he wanted to say something, then just muttered, "Yeah, well, you probably sucked at it too."

"Still do," I said, and for a heartbeat, the air between us felt normal.

We talked for a while, and I almost repeated what I said to Claire, and in the end, we stood up and hugged. A really enormous hug.

"Love you, old man," he said.

"I know." And I left to find my car and called Sophie. She said she would meet me downstairs.

I found Sophie sitting on the front steps of her building block, hugging her knees. She was the youngest, but grief had aged her faster than I wanted to admit.

"You okay, Soph?" I asked, easing down beside her.

She shook her head. "I hate it when people say that. Like, what do they think I'm supposed to say? Yeah, I'm fine, my mum's dead, thanks for asking?"

Her voice cracked on the last word, and my chest ached. I reached to put an arm around her, but she stiffened.

"Sorry," I murmured, pulling my arm back.

"It's not you, Dad. It's just sometimes I feel like I'm not allowed to be sad. Like, you're trying so hard to look better, and Claire's always telling me to be strong. And Daniel just yells at his Xbox. So, when am I supposed to cry?"

That broke me.

Because she was right.

Each of us was stumbling through his or her own storm, blind to the others.

"You can cry right now," I said softly.

She didn't, not fully, but she leaned into me.

And in that quiet moment, I realised this wasn't about me keeping Maureen alive in conversations or in my mind.

It was about making sure our kids didn't drown in the silence she left behind.

"Dad, can I ask you a question?"

"Sure sweetheart. Anything?"

"Will you remarry? Replace Mum?"

It took me by surprise, her question, but I was ready with an answer.

"Sophie, your mum will never be replaced. I realise that losing her will always be harder on you kids. You lost your *mother*—that's someone who cannot ever be replaced. I might find someone later in life, but that person will never, and I mean *never*, replace your mother. Do you understand what I am saying, baby?"

Sophie stood up, and so did I.

She threw her arms around me and just smiled and whispered in my ear: "Yes, I understand, Dad. Thanks for being honest and for being here for me. For us."

Later, when I went to bed, Maureen was there.

She didn't tease me.

She didn't make a joke.

Just whispered, "They need you more than they need me now. Remember, honey, you are now a single parent."

"I know I am, even if they' re grown adults. I am their single father now."

Maureen looked at me and smiled and just added: "And a damn good one at that."

And I knew she was right as I took off my jumper and closed my eyes to go to sleep, thinking of my children and my Maureen.

HIGH SCHOOL REUNION

Even with the progress I was making, it was still months before I admitted it to myself.

Maureen's voice filled the house with laughter again, her jokes were as sharp as ever, but at night… the bed was still a cavern. Empty. Cold. No matter how much she teased me from the other side, I couldn't ignore the gnawing hollow that came when the lights went out.

I tried distracting myself. I watched cricket reruns. I polished the car. I even organised the shed, which Maureen would have called a miracle of biblical proportion. But nothing dulled the truth: I wanted touch. Warmth. Companionship that wasn't spectral.

One night, while I was moping in my chair with a glass of red, Maureen's voice cut through like the crack of a whip: "Josh, love, you can't stay in this limbo forever. You're half-alive."

I groaned. "What am I supposed to do? Take up speed dating at the RSL?"

She chuckled, with the same low laugh that once made me fall for her in a Georgia Tech jumper. "Not speed dating. Online dating. Everyone does it now."

"Online dating?" I nearly choked. "Maureen, I don't even know how to upload a photo without Daniel's help."

"Well then, get help. But listen—use a recent photo, not one from 1987. No woman wants to swipe right on a mullet."

I laughed so hard my ribs hurt. "You're cruel."

"I'm honest. And you're adorable when you're flustered."

But then the laughter ebbed, and I felt the ache again. "I don't know how to be with anyone else," I admitted. "You're it, Maureen. You're the only one who's ever known me... properly."

For once, she didn't joke. "That's exactly why you can learn again. You did it once, love. You can do it again."

The next morning, as I checked my email, I found the answer. Buried between spam about discounted hearing aids and a subscription reminder for The Sydney Morning Herald, there it was:

Subject: *Northport High Alumni Reunion - You ' re Invited!*

I almost deleted it.

Who wanted to revisit pimples, polyester uniforms, and awkward slow dances?

But before I could hit the trash button, Maureen piped up: "Go."

I muttered, "No way. I'd rather re-roof the house in midsummer."

"Joshua," she said in that voice that always won arguments, "you need to put yourself in the path of people again. Start with people you already know. Even if you were a pimply mess back then."

"Thanks for the confidence boost."

"Always here to help."

I shook my head. "It's going to be weird. Everyone will ask about you."

"Let them. Tell them I'm still bossing you around."

I laughed. She wasn't wrong.

So that's how I found myself, two Saturdays later, standing in front of Northport High's gymnasium doors, heart hammering like I was about to sit my HSC all over again. I wore my decent blazer—the one Maureen always said made me look like I'd borrowed it from my dad—and my old Georgia Tech jumper tucked under it, for courage.

Inside, balloons sagged in the corners, the smell of reheated sausage rolls filled the air, and a DJ who looked too young to know vinyl blasted '80s hits as if he'd discovered them yesterday.

And there I was—40 years older, a little heavier, hair more salt than pepper—stepping back into the past.

I swore I heard Maureen whisper: "Go on, Josh. Live a little."

I looked around and saw that the gym was packed with ghosts of the living. Old classmates, a few teachers who looked as though they'd been preserved in formaldehyde, and a scattering of people whose faces I half-recognised but couldn't place. I did the polite nodding tour:

"Good to see you!"

"You haven't changed a bit!"

—lies, all of it.

I was halfway to the refreshment table when I heard someone call my name.

"Joshua?"

I turned. And for a second, the room tilted.

Rose Marie Thompson.

My first proper girlfriend, back when I thought love meant sweaty palms and saving up for movie tickets. We'd lost touch after high school—she'd gone to university in Melbourne, while I'd chased architecture and met a certain red-haired hurricane who became my Maureen.

Rose Marie stood there, wineglass in hand, with the kind of smile that punched through four decades like they were nothing. She had silver streaks in her hair now, laugh lines that told me she'd lived fully, but her eyes… they were exactly as I remembered.

"Rosie," I breathed, and immediately felt like a teenager again.

"Well," she said, tilting her head, "how have you been Joshua. I have not seen you in years. Not since the year we spent almost here weeks in detention after school."

I laughed so loudly people turned. "You remember that?"

"How could I forget? You were one crazy young man. I thought you were going to propose we skip the detention."

"Well I thought about it but chicken out at the end."

Behind me, I swear I heard Maureen whisper: "She's got your number, love."

Rose stepped closer.

"I'm sorry, I didn't mean to ambush you. It's just… it's been years. Decades."

I nodded.

"Too many. You look…" I stopped, fumbling. Complimenting women felt like a foreign language now. "…like life's treated you well."

She smiled softly, and for a moment there was a current between us—not the old teenage spark, but something gentler, steadier. A recognition.

We found a quiet corner and started catching up. Rose had been married, had kids, and lost her husband a few years back. Much like me.

"It's been lonely," she admitted. "My children keep telling me to 'get out there,' as if companionship is something you just order online."

I nearly spat out my drink. "That's what Maureen said!"

Rose blinked. "Maureen?"

I froze, then laughed it off. "My wife. She passed away not long ago. But she still, well, let's just say she still has opinions."

Rose's hand brushed mine.

"I'm sorry, Josh. I really am. But if she was anything like the girl you chose all those years ago, I can imagine she'd want you to keep living."

From somewhere over my shoulder, Maureen's voice teased: "I like her already. She gets me. How come you never told me about her?"

"Shush."

"What?" Rose asked.

I tried not to grin like a madman. "Oh nothing. Just muttering to myself."

We talked for nearly two hours, the hum of the reunion fading into the background noise. Rose told me about her garden, her grandkids, her retirement plans. I laughed, laughing properly, in a way I hadn't in months.

As the DJ cued up a slow song—something painfully cliché, like "Unforgettable"—Rose glanced at me. "Do you still dance?"

"Badly," I said.

She held out her hand. "Some things never change."

I hesitated, thinking of Maureen, of empty beds, of nights I'd whispered into shadows. Then I slipped my hand into hers.

And I swore, for a moment, I felt Maureen's voice in my ear: "Go on, Josh. Live. You've got my blessing."

So, I did.

The dance was awkward.

My shoes squeaked against the gym floor, and I was certain I looked like a malfunctioning wind-up toy.

But Rose Marie only laughed and guided me gently, like she had all those years ago when we were teenagers at our first school formal.

"You always overthink it," she said.

"I'm trying not to step on your toes."

"Josh, I've raised children. My toes are tougher than you think."

We both laughed, and for the first time in months, it wasn't bittersweet—it was simply good.

FIRST KISS

Over the next few weeks, Rose and I slipped into a kind of rhythm. Coffee time together, phone calls that stretched past midnight, short walks where we filled each other in on the decades we'd missed. It was cautious—two widowed souls testing the waters. We didn't call it 'dating.' We didn't call it anything.

We just were.

And every time I came home, I put my jumper on, and Maureen was there.

"Well," she teased one night as I hung up the phone, "aren't we the smooth talker? Three hours, Josh. That's longer than you ever lasted at a staff meeting."

I groaned. "She's easy to talk to, that's all."

"That's *something*," Maureen countered. "Don't hide behind excuses."

"I'm not hiding."

"You're absolutely hiding. You've built a fortress out of nostalgia and grief, and now someone's finally rattling the gates."

I rubbed my temples. "It feels wrong, Maureen. To enjoy this. To laugh with someone who isn't you."

Her voice softened. "It's not wrong. It's human. You loved me with everything you had. I know that. But I don't want to be your last chapter."

Jesus, that silenced me.

The following Sunday, Rose invited me over for lunch.

Her kitchen smelled like rosemary chicken, and she insisted on pouring me wine. We sat at her table, talking about everything from high school mischief to grandparenthood, and then, without thinking, I reached across and touched her hand.

It was small and tentative.

A brush of fingers. But it sent a shock through me.

Rose stared at me, but gently. "Josh… are you sure?"

I almost pulled back. Almost.

But then the memory of Maureen's voice slid into my ear, warm and certain: "Go on, love. She's not replacing me. She's reminding you how to live."

So, I didn't pull back.

We stayed like that, our hands resting together, while the world outside went on turning.

Later that night, I sat in my armchair, the Georgia Tech jumper hugging my shoulders. "Well?" I asked into the quiet.

"Well, what?" Maureen teased.

"You saw. You heard. What do you think?"

"No, Josh. I did not see. I heard nothing. You weren' t wearing the jumper, so I can' t tell you anything. Tell me what happened so I can answer your question."

I related what had transpired with as much detail and as honestly as possible.

"I think Rose Marie Thompson has good taste in men."

"Maureen…"

Her laughter softened into something like a sigh. "Josh, you're allowed to love again. It doesn't mean you love me less. It means I loved you well enough that your heart still works."

I leaned back, eyes stinging. "I don't know if I'm ready."

"You don't have to be ready," she said. "You just have to be willing."

That night, I slept easier. The bed was still empty, but not as cavernous.

Because somewhere out there, Rose Marie was sleeping too.

And maybe Maureen was right.

The next day I met Rosie for a coffee and boy was I in for a surprise!

"Josh, you've been buying me coffees, and we've gone out to restaurants for weeks," she said one afternoon as we walked along the river path. "It's my turn to cook for you. A proper dinner. No excuses."

I stammered something about not wanting to impose, but she gave me the look—the same one she used to give teachers when she wanted an extension on assignments. It still worked.

So, the following Saturday evening, I stood outside her house with a bottle of red in my hand, heart thudding like I was 17 again.

The moment she opened the door; I was struck dumb. Rose Marie wore a simple black dress, nothing extravagant, but it made her eyes brighter, her smile warmer.

"Damn, you look…" I began, then promptly forgot how sentences worked.

"Like someone who still knows how to shop?" she teased and ushered me inside.

Her dining table was set with candles.

Real candles, not the battery-powered ones my kids insisted I use after that one unfortunate tea-light incident.

The smell of garlic and herbs drifted from the kitchen.

"Roast lamb," she said proudly. "The old family recipe."

"I knew there was a reason I showed up," I quipped.

From somewhere near my ear, Maureen's voice cut in: "Smooth, Joshua. Real Casanova."

I almost choked on the air. I wasn't wearing my Georgia Tech jumper, so it had to be my guilty conscience speaking to me.

"Relax, Josh, relax," I told myself.

Dinner was wonderful.

We talked about the silly things—our first jobs, our disastrous attempts at gardening—and the heavier things, too.

She told me about her late husband, about how he used to sing loudly in the shower. I told her about Maureen's singing, how she could fold a fitted sheet properly, but claimed she'd invented her own 'system.'

Rose Marie laughed, a sound rich and genuine, and for a moment, I thought, *This feels like home.*

After the plates were cleared, she poured us each another glass of wine. We lingered, talking slower now, the candles burning lower as we sat on her sofa.

"Josh," she said softly, "I wasn't sure when I saw you at the reunion... if it would feel right. You know. Seeing you again."

I nodded. "I know the feeling."

"But it does," she whispered. "It feels right. Different, of course. We're different. But right."

I swallowed hard. My hands were shaking.

That was when I heard Maureen again, her voice low but firm: "Go on, Josh. Don't waste this moment."

I leaned across, my heart pounding. Rosie met me halfway.

The kiss was gentle, tentative.

Not a blazing teenage spark, but something deeper—a quiet affirmation that life could bloom again, even after loss.

When we finally drew back, I laughed nervously. "Well. That only took about 40 years."

Rose smiled. "Worth the wait."

I swear I felt Maureen's approval, like a hand on my shoulder, steady and sure.

That night, as I drove home, I realised something:

The emptiness was still there. Maureen would always be a part of me. But for the first time, the hollow didn't echo so painfully.

Because now, someone else's laughter might fill it.

WOLLONGONG

It wasn't simple. In fact, it was harder than I'd let on to anyone—even Rose Marie.

Each time we laughed together, each time I brushed her hand or kissed her goodnight, there was a sting of guilt that followed me home like a shadow. My chest ached with questions: *Am I betraying Maureen? Can I give Rose Marie the same love? Or am I just clinging to someone who reminds me I'm still alive?*

The worst part was that I didn't know the answer.

Maureen's voice, once so constant, grew quieter. At first, it was subtle. I'd come home after seeing Rose. I put on the jumper and expect her usual teasing commentary—Smooth move, Casanova—but I'd only hear silence.

"Maureen?" I whispered one night in the dimly lit lounge room.

For a long time, nothing.

Then, faintly, like an echo fading down a corridor: "I'm still here, Josh. Just not quite as much. You don't need me the same way anymore."

That rattled me more than anything. Because I needed her. I wanted her voice filling the silence, even if it meant I'd never move forward.

With Rose, it was different.

Gentle. Patient.

She didn't rush me.

She didn't demand labels or declarations.

We shared walks, dinners, evenings by her garden where she showed me which flowers bloomed even after frost.

"You're like these roses," she said one evening, holding a red blossom in her hand. "You think the season is over, but look—there's still life, still beauty."

I smiled, but inside I felt torn. Rose Marie was right.

And yet, wasn't it Maureen who had always been my rose?

That night, when Rose kissed me under the garden lights, it felt warm and real… but later, lying alone in bed, I whispered into the dark: "Maureen, help me. I don't know how to do this."

This time, there was only silence. No matter how long I waited.

Weeks passed. Rose and I grew closer.

The kids grew used to her presence, though Claire still gave me that look—part protective daughter, part resigned adult who knew her dad was stubborn but deserving of happiness.

And me?

I wrestled with myself daily.

I'd smile with Rose and ache for Maureen in the same breath. I'd hold Rose's hand while feeling the ghost of Maureen's fingers slipping through mine.

It was exhausting, loving the past and reaching for the future at once.

One night after dinner at Rose's, I came home, poured myself a Harvey Bristol Cream sherry, put on the jumper and sat in the recliner.

"I kissed her again tonight," I said aloud. "And it felt good. But it hurt too. Like I'm leaving you behind."

The silence stretched, heavy.

Then, at last, finally, Maureen's voice came, soft and far away: "You're not leaving me, love. You're carrying me with you. Always. But it's time you carried someone else, too. That doesn't erase me. It adds to you."

I swallowed hard, tears running freely. "I'm scared, Maureen."

"I know. But you'll be alright. You've got her. And you'll always have me—not as a voice in your ear, but as a part of you. Forever."

And then silence.

Real silence.

I sat there all night, in my jumper, terrified and comforted in equal measure. I knew she was right.

Maureen was fading.

Not gone, never gone, but stepping back. Leaving the room.

The next morning, Rose called.

"I was thinking," she said, her voice light but hopeful. "Would you like to take a trip with me? Somewhere quiet. Just the two of us. No past, no distractions. Just us."

For a long moment, I couldn't speak.

My throat tightened, my heart raced.

A trip meant choosing.

A trip meant stepping out of limbo and into something new.

Finally, I said, "Yes."

And as I hung up, I realised I hadn't put on the jumper and asked Maureen's for her opinion first.

That was the hardest, and the most freeing, moment of all.

We went to the coast. Wollongong.

Not far, just an hour᾽s drive or so , but far enough that the air smelled different, the horizon opened up, and the tide seemed to wash clean the weight I'd been carrying.

Rosie booked a little seaside cottage—white weatherboards with blue shutters, a place you'd imagine on a postcard.

When we arrived, she slipped her arm through mine and said, "This feels like the right place to begin something."

Her words made me both swell and ache.

That first evening, we walked along the beach barefoot, shoes dangling from our hands. The sand was cool, the surf whispered in, and Rosie's hair whipped around her face in the breeze.

She laughed, trying to tame it. "Well, this isn't glamorous."

"It's perfect," I said. And I meant it.

But inside, I still felt the pull of Maureen.

Her hand in mine on other beaches, her laughter carried by other winds. It was like walking with two women at once: one beside me, one inside me.

Later, after dinner on the cottage deck—grilled fish, simple salad, a bottle of chilled white wine—Rosie reached across the table and touched my hand.

"You're somewhere else," she said softly.

"I'm here," I replied. But even I heard the hesitation.

She nodded. "I know it's difficult. I'd never ask you to forget her, Josh. But I will ask you to let yourself be here, with me, too."

The honesty in her eyes nearly undid me.

I wanted to promise her everything. But all I could do was whisper, "I'm trying."

That night, lying awake in the little bedroom with the waves pounding faintly beyond the window, I clutched my jumper.

I looked across at Rosie sleeping, and I slowly got up and went to the balcony and put on the jumper.

"I don't know how to do this," I murmured into the dark.

For the first time in weeks, I heard her voice—faint, distant, but warm. "You're already doing it, love. You're loving again. And that's all I ever wanted for you."

Tears spilled down my cheeks. "I miss you."

"And you always will. But I'm proud of you, Josh. So proud."

Then silence.

It was a gentle silence, not the haunting absence I'd feared.

It was as if she'd finally settled into her place, no longer hovering, but folded into me. Like the tide pulling back, leaving the sand glistening.

I slipped back into the little bedroom after the balcony and sat on the edge of the bed for a long time, the jumper heavy in my hands. Rosie turned toward me, breathing slowly, and even in the dim light, I could see the silhouette of her face and the small, steady rise of her chest. For a moment I simply watched her—the steady, ordinary beauty of a woman who had been with me.

She stirred and opened her eyes. "Are you okay?" she whispered.

"I think so," I said. "I'm… scared that I'll ruin this somehow."

The words came out small, ridiculous for a grown man, but true.

She reached for me without hurry.

Her fingers found the back of my neck and drew me down until our foreheads met. There was no hurry in it, no searching for answers, only the warmth of two people leaning into something fragile and hopeful. We talked in breaths and half-smiles, traded the small confessions that make strangers into companions: the silly things we were embarrassed about, the quiet things that made us ache.

Then we kissed.

A long, gentle thing that tasted of sea air and wine and the salt of my own tears. It wasn't desperate or clumsy. It was careful, as if we both knew we were tending something that deserved gentleness. Her hands were patient; mine learned to be patient in return. Clothes were set aside like the slight obstacles they were; not with urgency but with a kind of reverence that made the ordinary feel sacred.

We lay together, bodies aligned but unpressured and lingered the first time and yet somehow as if remembering. I remembered the weight of her hand on my chest, the easy way she breathed my name, the soft laugh we shared when I said something embarrassingly earnest.

It was tender in ways that surprised me, not flashy or forceful, but full: a joining that soothed as much as it thrilled.

There were moments I thought of Maureen—a flash of a laugh, the shape of a familiar shoulder—and then Rosie would brush my hair from my forehead, and the ache would soften.

It didn't disappear; it simply became part of the quiet.

What happened between us that night was not an erasure.

It was a sign of approval.

It was permission from one human to another to be held, to love each other and to not hold back.

Afterwards, we lay with our hands linked, listening to the house breathe and the ocean murmur beyond the window. I felt oddly whole and oddly precarious at once; the two feelings sat beside each other like guests at a table.

Rosie curled into me and, in that small, steady warmth, something inside me loosened—not replaced but given space to be larger and kinder than it had been when it was only grief.

When sleep finally came, it was not the restless dozing I'd become used to. It was a deep, honest sleep that felt less like forgetting and more like choosing to wake differently.

The next morning, Rose and I sat with our coffees, the sea mist rising around us. She looked at me over the rim of her cup and smiled—not a youthful, giddy smile, but one that held patience, kindness, and promise.

And I realised: I could love her.

Not as I loved Maureen, because no one could replace that, but in a new way. A way that honoured where I'd been and where I might still go.

I reached out, took her hand, and said, "Let's see where this leads, Rose."

She squeezed my fingers. "I'd like that."

And in that moment, I didn't hear Maureen's voice.

But I felt her blessing.

Quiet, steady, eternal.

FAMILY CHRISTMAS

Christmas used to be Maureen's masterpiece. She loved it all. Decorating the tree, cooking pork, ham. beef, prawns, turnkey, you name it, and it was on the table. Singing carols off-key but louder than any choir on the telly.

After she passed, I thought I'd never stomach Christmas again, the first one being the toughest.

But here I was, a year and a bit later, standing in my lounge room as the smell of roast ham filled the air, fairy lights twinkled on the tree, and laughter spilled from every corner.

It wasn't just my kids this year either. I made sure that Rosie brought her brood too.

Her two daughters, their husbands, and a scattering of grandchildren who were already trying to unravel my carefully wrapped gifts.

It was chaos. It was loud. And, to my surprise, it felt good.

Not perfect, for nothing without Maureen could be perfect, but good.

The dining table groaned under the weight of food.

Roast potatoes, ham glazed in honey, trifle so colourful it looked like it belonged in a science experiment. I carved the ham while Daniel poured drinks, Sophie bossed around the younger kids, and Claire—still cautious around Rose, though less sharp than before—arranged cutlery like she was laying down a battle plan.

Rosie sat beside me, her hand brushing mine now and then, grounding me. She'd brought her famous lemon slice again, though she insisted it wasn't Christmas-worthy. "They'll eat it before the pudding," she said and she was right.

At one point, I looked around the table, at my children and hers, at the noise and the mismatched decorations, and thought: *This is what surviving grief looks like. It's messy. It's stitched together from old memories and new ones. But it's alive.*

Of course, no family gathering was complete without an awkward question or two.

We'd just sat down, plates piled high, when one of Rose's grandkids, a boy with too much energy and too little tact, piped up: "So, are you two getting married or what?"

The room froze.

Forks paused mid-air.

Sophie nearly dropped her gravy.

Claire's eyes widened.

Daniel coughed into his drink.

I stared at the boy, gobsmacked. "Married?"

"Yeah," he said, shrugging as only a child can. "You're always together. Mum says you hold hands like teenagers. If you're not going to marry, are you going to move in together?"

Rose Marie turned pink.

I nearly choked on my ham.

Somewhere in the back of my head, I swear I heard Maureen's laughter—not cruel, but warm, as if she were pulling up a chair to enjoy the show.

"Well," I started, fumbling for words, "that's a very direct question."

The boy grinned. "That's what Mum says too. I'm direct."

Rosie placed her hand over mine under the table.

Her touch steadied me.

I smiled at the boy, then at the entire table, and said, "We're happy the way we are."

Rosie squeezed my hand, nodded, and added, "Exactly. We don't need titles or rings to know what this is. We have each other. And that's enough."

There was a pause.

Then Sophie, bless her heart, raised her glass. "To Dad and Rose. May they stay happy, exactly how they are."

Everyone followed suit, glasses clinking.

Even Claire lifted hers, though she gave me a look that said, *'We're going to talk about this later.'*

The boy? He just grinned. "Cool. Can I have more pudding now?"

The tension broke, laughter bubbled, and the room filled with the warmth of people choosing joy over judgment.

Daniel leaned toward me. "Nice save, Dad."

I smirked. "You doubted me?"

"Always," he said.

After dinner, the grandkids staged a nativity play with tea towels for shepherd hats and a plastic doll for baby Jesus. The adults sat around sipping wine, the fairy lights blinking lazily in the background. I caught myself holding Rose's hand openly now.

At one point, I slipped into the pantry off the kitchen to catch my breath.

Old habits—stepping away when the noise got too much.

The Christmas tree sparkled, and I felt that familiar tug in my chest.

"Maureen," I whispered, "I hope you see this. I hope you're smiling."

For a long moment, there was nothing but the hum of conversation behind me.

Then, faintly, like the rustle of wrapping paper, I swear I heard "I'm here, love. Always. Merry Christmas."

It wasn't the constant voice of before.

It was softer now, more of a blessing than a presence.

And for once, that was enough.

Later, as the night wound down and coats were gathered, Sophie hugged Rose tightly. "Thanks for making Christmas feel like Christmas again."

Rose's eyes welled. "That means the world."

Claire lingered at the door, watching us.

Then, almost grudgingly, she said, "Dad, I can see you're happy. And Mum would've wanted that. I'll get used to it. Just don't forget her."

My throat tightened. "Claire, I couldn't forget your mother if I lived a thousand years."

She nodded, hugged me quickly, and walked out.

Progress.

When the house was finally quiet, Rose and I sat side by side on the sofa, surrounded by torn wrapping paper and the faint smell of pork crackling.

"You handled that question well," she teased.

I chuckled. "I was about to hide under the table."

She leaned her head on my shoulder. "I'm glad we don't need to rush. I like us just as we are."

I kissed the top of her head. "So do I."

And as the lights twinkled and the night settled, I realised that Christmas didn't feel like a monument to what I'd lost anymore. It felt like a bridge—between the love that had shaped me and the love that was helping me live again.

POSTSCRIPT

If you'd told me a year ago that I'd survive any Christmas without Maureen, I would've laughed in your face. The bitter laugh you use when you don't believe a word.

Christmas was her holiday.

She lived for it. She'd start playing Christmas music in November just to get a rise out of me.

So, when she died, I figured Christmas had died with her.

But there I was, this past December, ham carving knife in one hand, Rose Marie's fingers tangled with mine under the table, grandchildren, not even mine, technically, tearing into gifts like piranhas, and my own kids pretending not to be mortified by the chaos.

And do you know what?

It wasn't terrible. It wasn't even sad, not all the way through.

It was messy, loud, awkward, and strangely wonderful.

Turns out grief doesn't cancel Christmas.

It just rewrites the carols a little.

I've learned a few things along the way.

First, ghosts make terrible relationship coaches. Don't get me wrong, Maureen's advice was invaluable—"Use a current photo for online dating, Josh, not the one with your mullet" still rings in my ears—but try explaining to your kids that you're dating again because your dead wife told you to. It doesn't go over well. Claire called a psychiatrist.

Second, love doesn't follow rules. I thought I'd feel nothing close to what I felt with Maureen. And maybe I won't—not in the same way. But Rose Marie has taught me that love can grow again, differently, in soil you thought was barren. It's not a copy. It's not a replacement. It's something new, tender, and stubborn, like one of those roses in her garden that insists on blooming after frost.

Third, family will always ask the awkward questions. "Are you getting married?" "Are you moving in together?" "Are you holding hands under the table?" Yes, yes, and none of your business. Well, maybe not the marriage part. For now, Rose and I are happy exactly as we are. Rings and joint bank accounts don't define us. We're not trying to fit into a Hallmark movie; we're just trying to live.

Do I still talk to Maureen? Sometimes, but I don't need to put on the Georgia Tech jumper. Not as often as before. I think she is on my mind now.

At first, her voice was everywhere, filling the silence, correcting me, laughing at me, telling me when I was being a coward. Slowly, though, she's stepped back. These days it's more like a blessing than a conversation—a warmth in the room when I need it most.

And I think that's how it should be.

I loved Maureen with everything I had, and I always will. That doesn't stop just because she isn't here to do a terrific Christmas meal anymore. But I can love Rose Marie too, without betraying Maureen. It took me months of guilt, a few beers, Harvey Bristols, and awkward family dinners to believe that, but it's true. Love isn't a one-time-only ticket. It's not a pie you divide between people. It's a garden—and if you water it, it keeps growing.

Sometimes sideways.

Sometimes where you least expect it.

But it grows.

Of course, none of this means it's easy. There are still nights I reach across the bed, half-asleep, expecting Maureen to be there. There are songs I can't listen to without turning into a puddle.

And there are moments with Rose where I laugh so hard, I feel guilty for enjoying it.

But grief and joy, I've realised, aren't enemies. They're twins. They are like a stereo. They live side by side, elbowing each other like siblings who can't share the back seat. One day grief takes the wheel; the next day joy does. And now and then, they let me drive.

So where does that leave me now?

I'm still a widower.

That title doesn't go away.

But I'm also a man who holds hands at Christmas dinner, who kisses Rose Marie goodnight, who lets his children see that happiness after loss isn't betrayal—it's survival.

Maureen once told me, back when we were both facing our cancers, "If I go first, don't you dare mope around forever. Find someone. Love again. Be ridiculous again."

I thought she was joking.

Turns out she was dead serious. (Pun intended—she'd laugh at that.)

This Christmas, as I sat at the table with Rosie, my children, her children, her grandchildren tearing into the pudding like it was treasure, I felt something I didn't think I'd feel again: peace. Not because the ache was gone; it never will be, but because laughter surrounded it, softened by fresh memories being made.

Grief taught me the value of silence.

Love, both old and new, taught me the value of noise.

And now I think I need both.

So, here's my closing thought, dear reader, from one stumbling, half-grieving, half-hopeful man to anyone who might need it:

Don't be afraid to laugh when your heart is broken. Don't be afraid to love when your hands are still trembling. And don't let anyone tell you happiness after loss is wrong.

Because if you're lucky, like me, you'll find that the people you've loved, and lost, aren't gone at all.

They're right there in the room, rolling their eyes at your bad dancing, whispering "I told you so," and blessing every ridiculous step you take forward.

And with that, from me, from Rose, and, in her own bossy way, from Maureen as well, we say: *Live, love and repeat.*

ABOUT THE AUTHOR

José F. Nodar is an Australian Cuban author, reviewer, and literary entrepreneur based in Spring Farm, NSW. He is the founder of Quick Story Tales Online and World Book Reviews, initiatives supporting and promoting both emerging and established authors worldwide.

José's writing blends humour, sentiment, and quiet realism, often drawing from the landscapes and community spirit of regional New South Wales. His fiction, including Whispers from My Wife, The Northport Coffee Group, and Stories to Share with My Partner Collection, explores universal themes of love, loss, and rediscovery.

When not writing, José can be found reading at a local café, walking along Spring Farm's footpaths, or championing local authors and creative groups through interviews and newsletters.

Please visit https://worldbookreviews.com.au/ and let me know what you thought of this book of short stories and poetry.

Good, bad, or indifferent, I will always welcome your honest opinion.

Send me an email at info@jfnodar.com.au

Thank you for your purchase!

OTHER BOOKS BY JOSÉ F. NODAR

Novels in English

- The Danny Monk Trilogy
- Books, Pens & Larceny
- Mending Hearts at Crystal Cove
- A Love Finally Spoken
- The Mallard E. Benson Trilogy
- The Girl Who Didn't Come Home
- The Ones That Got Away
- The Ghost We Owe

Mystery

- The Ghost Detective's First Case
- The Northport Coffee Group

Romance

- The Teacher's Assistant
- A Night of Love
- Maybe This Is Everything
- Love in Stereo
- When Love Remembers

Science Fiction & Fantasy

- The Universe Between Us
- The Time Bus
- The Last Light of Aurethis

Children

- The Compass Legacy
- The Hamster Who Whispered Back

Humour

- SEX

Anthologies of Stories and Poetry

- Quick Stories & Poems Volume I
- Quick Stories & Poems Volume 2
- Quick Stories & Poems Volume 3

Collections of Stories and Poetry

- Stories to Share with My Partner Book 1
- Stories to Share with My Partner Book 2
- Stories to Share with My Partner Book 3
- Stories to Share with My Partner Book 4
- Stories to Share with My Partner Book 5
- Stories to Share with My Partner Book 6
- Stories to Share with My Partner Book 7
- Stories to Share with My Partner Book 8

- Stories to Share with My Partner Book 9

- Stories to Share with My Partner Book 10

- Stories to Share with My Partner Book 11

- Stories to Share with My Partner Book 12

Libros en Español

La Trilogía de Danny Monk
- Un Amor Expresado

- Reparando Corazones en Crystal Cove

- Un Amor Finalmente Declarado

Colecciones de Cuentos y Poemas
- Cuentos Para Compartir con Mi Pareja Libro 1

- Cuentos Para Compartir con Mi Pareja Libro 2

- Cuentos Para Compartir con Mi Pareja Libro 3

Ciencia Ficción y Fantasía
- El Autobús del Tiempo